W9-BMZ-818

October Song

BEVERLY LEWIS

October Song

BETHANYHOUSE

Published by Bethany House Publishers
A Ministry of Bethany Fellowship International
11400 Hampshire Avenue South
Bloomington, Minnesota 55438

ISBN 0-7642-2588-X

Dedication

◆

To Martha Nelson
For all the years of our friendship.
Here's to many more!

By Beverly Lewis

*with David Lewis

Beverly Lewis was born in the heart of Pennsylvania Dutch country. She fondly recalls her growing-up years, and due to a keen interest in her mother's Plain family heritage, many of Beverly's books are set in Lancaster County.

A former schoolteacher, Bev is a member of The National League of American Pen Women—the Pikes Peak branch—and the Society of Children's Book Writers and Illustrators. Her bestselling books are among the C. S. Lewis Noteworthy List Books, and both *The Postcard* and *Annika's Secret Wish* have received Silver Angel Awards. Bev and her husband have three children and make their home in Colorado.

Visit Beverly's Web site at: *www.BeverlyLewis.com*.

Author's Note

The lore of the Plain people continues to draw me back to my family heritage. For that reason, the stories in this volume sprang up from fertile Lancaster County soil indeed. Just as an Amish quilt is defined by motif, color, and design, so the following narratives are linked closely by setting, character, and theme—interconnected by common threads—a chronological tale in three parts.

Abundant pleas have come from my devoted readers who, since the publication of *The Shunning* and subsequent novels, have continued to inquire of characters such as Katie and Dan, the Wise Woman, Bishop John and Mary, Rachel and Philip, Sarah Cain, and Lydia Cottrell.

I, too, had been wondering about each of them and what has been happening in their lives. So it is my delight to present this story collection with endless appreciation to my wonderful editor, Barb Lilland, whose perspective and insight are invaluable. Special thanks to my "first editor" and husband, Dave, whose keen eye and ear are always an encouragement and help to me. Finally, to my dear parents, Herb and Jane Jones, whose call to minister in the "Heart of Pennsylvania Dutch Country" is the reason I was blessed to have grown up in this lovely, verdant region in the first place.

Contents

◆

PART I

Hickory Hollow

The smell of woodsmoke hung in the air as crows
caw-cawed back and forth overhead. A bird sang out
a low, throaty series of notes and flew away. . . . So
isolated was the area that not even the smallest mark
on the Lancaster map betrayed the existence of
Hickory Hollow—home to two hundred and
fifty-three souls.

—from *The Shunning*

The Reunion

Forgetting those things which are behind, and reaching forth unto those things which are before . . .

—*Philippians 3:13*

A little over a year has passed since I stood with my beloved Daniel at the wedding altar, reciting my vows in the meetinghouse down the road. We're happily settled into marriage, and our home is located within walking distance from the outskirts of Hickory Hollow.

The tiny Amish village—*ach*, but a slight wrinkle on the map—wears a good many faces with the turning of the seasons. I'm ever so grateful to be living this close to the hollow, where I can still glimpse Amish children dashing across snow-laden mule roads in winter, heading to one frozen pond or another, skating till the cold comes a-creepin' up, nipping at their noses.

'Course, springtime and summer follow, sooner or later, along with flowering cherry trees and dogwoods, all decked out in the season's finest. Frivolity and fun are written all over the faces of youngsters as they ride scooters or roller-skate home after school. Young men of courting age offer quiet, yet eager, smiles to *perty* girls at Sunday night singings, showin' off their shiny black open buggies hitched to nimble stallions.

But, of all the seasons, autumn is the one I love best. The months of September and October, with bustling days of digging and marketing potatoes. Gatherin' corn, too. Men work long and hard, fillin' up silos. We women keep our hands busy with the inside chores of cannin' vegetables. Everything from apple butter to zucchini.

Along with the harvest comes fall housecleaning and oodles of mending. And evening hayrides now 'n' then, the harvest moon plump and orange in the sky. Daniel said here the other day that we oughta invite several of our couple friends over "after the hayride come this Friday night." His blue eyes shone with the idea. "We'll make some pineapple ice cream, too."

'Course, I was all for it. "Ice cream and Mamma's sugar cookies," I decided.

Honestly, we've made a good many Mennonite friends in our new church community. Almost enough to make up for the loss of my Amish kinfolk, I'm sometimes tempted to think.

Yet no matter how satisfying our newfound acquaintances, no one will ever take the place of my dear adoptive parents and brothers. Not the whole lot of aunts, uncles, and cousins neither. And there's dear Mary Stoltzfus—the young Amishwoman I grew up with—now happily married to Hickory Hollow's bishop, John Beiler. I wouldn't know from Mary's lips just how cheery she is, though. Our paths, hers and mine, don't cross much anymore. Not since my shunning.

I don't rightly know how long it's been since I stepped foot in the old farmhouse where I grew up. Not that my heart doesn't yearn for my dear ones. I'm just not welcome amongst the People, and I wouldn't think of stirrin' up more trouble than has already been done.

I *have* talked to Mamma by phone sometimes, when she's off tending to quilt tables at Central Market, downtown Lancaster. When it's possible, and there's a lull, she'll slip away to a pay phone and call. But those times are few and far between. More often than not, she sends cards and letters, even though I just live on the outskirts of the hollow.

On two separate occasions here lately, I've walked down Hickory Lane to visit the Wise Woman—Mamma's aunt Ella Mae Zook—under the covering of night. The elderly widow is my spiritual mother. Just last year she led me in the sinner's prayer. In the stillness of her living room, I found forgiveness of sin through faith in the Lord Jesus. My heart had been longing for that moment my whole life.

"Aw, Katie, my dear girl, time just seems to evaporate when we get together, ain't so?" Ella Mae says, her head just a-bobbin' up and down.

The Wise Woman knows, without a doubt, the joys of friendship. *Jah,* Ella Mae understands fully that time and distance mean little when it comes to family connections.

"We're like squares on a quilt," I tell her, sipping herbal tea in Ella Mae's dimly lit kitchen. "Always connected, we are, no matter."

No matter.

Pondering that, I truly wish something could be done, something within my power, about my present spiritual stand and my former church, the Old Order. Mamma's wanted so

17

much for us to visit, somehow or other. I'm perty sure my father's the one who's nixed the notion. Fact is, he follows the letter of the law, Dat does. He's strongly opposed to breaking bread—eating and talking together as if nothing's wrong—with either my husband or me, both of us under the *Bann* and *Meinding* as former church members.

Guess I can't blame him, though I've heard tell of a good many Amish families—none from the Hickory Hollow church district, but other places all the same—who bend the rules a bit for the sake of family ties.

Not Samuel Lapp. He's kept his silence toward me since that cold autumn Sunday, the day my shunning officially began, showing no interest in reaching out to me whatsoever as Mamma has. Nary a phone call or the shortest note in the mail. None of that.

Even my married brother, Elam, and his wife, Annie—Dan's sister—thought enough to send a Christmas card. At the bottom of the card, though, Elam scrawled these words: *We pray both you and Dan will be true-hearted and take the shunning seriously, repent, and return to your contract with God and the church.*

Yet another opportunity for my big brother to admonish us about our sin of breaking our baptismal vows, leaving the Amish for a less rigid fellowship of Christians, a church where salvation by grace is preached from the pulpit. But a church, nonetheless, that allows electricity and automobiles—a sin and a shame in the eyes of the Old Order.

On my knees, at age nineteen, I gave my heartfelt vow to be true to God and the Amish church. Having grown up Old Order, I was fully aware of the seriousness of such a kneeling oath—a lifetime pact with the Almighty—both then and now. I *have* kept my vow to God—even more so, I should say, since giving my heart fully to the Lord Jesus.

Will Dat ever forgive me?

To keep from frettin', I think on more practical things and set to housecleaning for our Friday company. Even so, Dat's rejection of me, his unforgiving spirit, casts its long shadow over my life. . . .

◆

After lunch Katie made a quick trip to the grocery store for a few items. Store visits took some getting used to. On the farm, the necessary ingredients for most recipes were usually on hand in storage bins down in the cold cellar of Dat's old farmhouse. Since marrying Dan Fisher, she no longer grew *all* their produce, due to limited space in their yard, but she tended a small vegetable garden. And no longer was there any barn choring to be done, but who missed milkin' cows twice a day? What she *did* miss were the farm surroundings, the smells—sweet ripening grapes, newly mown hay, honeysuckle on the vine—and the sound of crickets *chir-r-rupping* in summer and the gentle creaking of windmills. Most of all, fellowship with the People.

More than ever, Katie found time for taking in sewing now and then, doing her own embroidery and mending, singing and playing guitar, cooking for and doting on her husband. Sometimes, while searching the Scriptures, she lost track of time, soaking up God's Word like a bone-dry sponge.

Dan contented himself as a draftsman by day and a musician by night and weekend; at such times he composed hymn arrangements for their guitar duets. Often, the newlyweds were invited to play in home gatherings, as well as at their church. All for the glory of God.

While driving over the back roads to the store, Katie felt ever so confident today. More so than usual. The Lord had been so good to give her a godly and loving husband, the man of her dreams since girlhood. She sang as she traveled, the sun shining down all round her, birds flitting from tree to tree, warbling an October song.

Just as she made the turn onto the gravel, Katie spied a distant horse and gray buggy coming down the road. A lump rose in her throat at the familiar sight, but she quickly dismissed the feeling, despite the tug at her heart.

Once inside the store, she gathered up necessary ingredients for the age-old cookie recipe—granulated sugar, cream of tartar, vanilla, and sweet milk. She checked her list before going to stand in line.

It was while Katie waited to pay for her few items that her father came into the store, big as you please. All at once, the wind fell out of her sails, seein' Dat for the first time since her return to Lancaster County last year. Truly, she felt lost. Yet she waved, even stepped forward slightly in anticipation. In that split second, as their eyes met and held briefly, he turned away, brushing past her.

She could scarcely breathe. And the tears . . . well, her eyes clouded up so much she had to dig in her pocketbook for a tissue.

'Tis better to forgive than to hold a grudge. . . .

How many times had Dat said that over the years? Her father had taught by example that "mercy bestowed upon a neighbor was grace handed down from almighty God." But, then, Katie wasn't just any neighbor. Having been raised in a strict Amish family, she'd run off from the People in willful disobedience—in search of fancy things—and returned home claiming to have become a Christian. Then, of all things, she had married an excommunicated Amishman, now a Mennonite.

Dat always embraced the belief that none can corrupt and leaven a person more than one's own spouse or children. 'Specially if such were wayward sinners, as she was in the eyes of the Old Order community. Dat truly believed that the shun was instituted to "make ashamed unto betterment of life," according to Menno Simons, the leader of persecuted Anabaptists during the sixteenth century.

Dat continues to shame me, hoping I'll come to my senses. The thought nagged at Katie as she paid the cashier and hurried out of the store. She fully understood her father's motive—no getting round that. Still, the sting of rejection bore deep inside. She couldn't help but think . . . *wish* she might've spent more time in the barn with Dat while growin' up, getting to know him better. 'Course, there were plenty of good memories, no denying that.

Take the time he'd helped her husk a full barrel of corn. "Such a lot of work for one little girl," he said all serious-like. But then his ruddy face burst into a rare smile.

"Aw, Dat, you don't hafta help me . . . I'm a big girl now."

He looked into the barrel and picked up several cobs of corn, letting them fall through his callused fingers. "I daresay you'll have these husked come suppertime." He paused, then asked, "Why ain't Mamma or Mary Stoltzfus out here helpin' ya?"

"Mamma's making stew for supper, and Mary's sewin' her first stitches on a quilt today, that's what."

Dat shook his head. "Seems a downright shame for you to be out here chorin' all alone." He picked up another cob and this time husked it quick as a wink, then another.

At the time, she wondered why Dat wasn't needed out in the field or the barn. Her brothers would surely wonder where he was, what Dat was doin' husking corn with their baby sister. But she just kept on reachin' for more cobs out of the barrel.

So did Dat. He made it seem so commonplace, as if he didn't have a dozen other more important tasks at the moment.

In the end, Mamma was surprised at such speedy work. Still, Katie never told on Dat, so to speak, that he'd wandered into the backyard for a spell, doing women's work with his wee daughter.

Another time she'd stood near the house watching her father and Elam cut down a diseased tree with a two-man cross-cut saw, across the barnyard near the shed. Never once in her short life had she heard him cuss, not even when his hand was cut nearly clean through by the saw. Dat had come close to bleeding to death that day. He would've, too, if it hadn't been for Mamma sending Elam down the road to use the telephone—the devil's instrument—at their Mennonite cousins' house. All the while Dat was steadfast, honorable, not one to rant and rail like Katie might've if the accident had happened to her, if *her* blood was drainin' too fast out of her body.

Fact was, Dat had a kind of inner strength Katie never quite understood. Something bigger than himself. Something that kept him firm on his feet when life got to be rough going.

Dat . . . What on earth could a girl do 'bout a man who'd been such a wonderful-*gut* part of your life? A man clad in old work trousers, patched at the knees, wearing muddy chorin' boots all day long, his ever-present straw hat perched atop his head, talking Dutch to the cows at milking, reading the German Bible to his children every night, teaching the ways of the Lord and the People. A man who, though prone to wrath when things weren't goin' his way under his own roof (under God), often held Mamma in his arms when she wasn't feeling quite up to snuff. What could you do 'bout a man like that, who put the fear of God in you when anger and rebellion a-kindled deep in your soul? A man who was just as strong-willed as you, a faithful man who stuck by the church's ordinances when you hid your banned guitar in the haymow and sang forbidden songs, then went off in search of your birth mother, breaking his and Mamma's heart? What could you do when you loved this man beyond words and prayed every day that God might make it possible for you to find the path back to his heart?

"One day it'll be so," Katie promised herself. One day she would talk openly with Dat. Come what may.

That night she lay awake, aware of her own beating heart, recalling her fleeting, yet painful encounter with Dat. His refusal to acknowledge her—instead looking away and passing her without so much as "Hullo." As she had for many months, she felt that something big was missing in her otherwise happy life. Something awful big.

23

"What is it, Katie?" Dan whispered next to her.

"My father . . . I saw him at the store today."

Dan drew her near.

"He turned his back on me." She fought the tears. "It's the first time since . . ."

"I know," Dan said. "I understand. . . ."

◆

Katie did a wise thing and paid a visit to Ella Mae the next evening after sundown. Pouring out her soul, Katie told her great-aunt that she couldn't possibly "make things right" with the People, confessing the way the church required of shunned members. Salvation through grace had been the longed-for missing link in her life, so how could she think of renouncing the God-given joy and forgiveness of sin, and offer repentance for having left the Amish church? Doing so would mean taking giant steps backward, according to the Scriptures. And what of her music ministry? Dan, too, had been called of God to do the work of the Kingdom. No, she could not—*would not*—forsake the Lord and the Gospel to regain her father's affections.

Ella Mae agreed wholeheartedly. "You're right as can be, Katie. Followin' Jesus sometimes calls for letting go of the past." The older woman sighed heavily, reaching for her handkerchief. "Ach, your father misses you so. I'm sure of it."

"Hard to believe," whispered Katie.

Ella Mae wiped her eyes and went on. "Why, on the Sunday the membership met to vote on casting you out of the fellowship, I saw with my own eyes how hard it was on Samuel Lapp. Honest to goodness, he had a quiver in his lip, he was sore pained by it all. The shun hurts us all, no getting round that."

So her father had been torn in two, just as Mamma was, along with other members of the Lapp family. The whole church district, really, according to Ella Mae.

"Nothing can ease my pain," Katie confessed.

The Wise Woman nodded, her eyes bright with tears. "You must be takin' it to the Lord, Katie. He's our great burden bearer."

Ella Mae was right. Trusting the heavenly Father for His will and way was best. More than ever, Katie was grateful for her relative's listening ear and compassionate heart. And she told Ella Mae so before slippin' out of the *Dawdi Haus* and into the night.

◆

Katie *did* take her burden to the Lord. But it was downright difficult, 'specially following the get-together with their friends. The subject of Eli—Katie's middle brother—and his soon-to-be wedding to a cousin of Mary, now the bishop's wife, came up midway through the evening.

"Eli's getting married. . . ? *When?*" she spluttered.

"Three weeks from Saturday" came the reply.

Why hasn't Mamma told me? she wondered, but she knew why. Truth was, shunned folk weren't invited to weddings.

Didn't matter if they were kin or not. No wedding invitation would be coming her way.

The old rush of sadness at the estrangement from family and close friends threatened to swallow Katie up.

Dan must've sensed something. "We'll buy a nice wedding gift," he said, reaching for her hand.

"Jah," she whispered. "We will."

◆

Out in their pumpkin patch the next day, Katie, along with her nearest neighbor, picked the nicest plump pumpkins. In spite of the warmth of the sun's rays, she felt the slightest nip in the air. It held the promise of a cold snap, perhaps, yet she was hopeful for a few more pleasant and sunny days ahead before frost-on-the-pumpkin time.

Remembering autumn days gone by, days that included her older brothers, Elam, Eli, and Benjamin—Dat and Mamma, too—Katie thought fondly of them, the whole family making butter by hand in the evening. The boys liked to make such a contest of it. A game, really. They actually timed their turns at the churn, giving each other only ten minutes, no more, laughing and poking fun all the while. Katie was scarcely old enough to steady the churn, so was given only a few minutes, if that.

"Ach, now, be fair," Mamma chided from her lawn chair, watching from afar.

If churning butter happened to be on a day when chores were caught up, Dat might linger near, squatting in the grass near Mamma, serious as ever, though seemingly enjoying the quietude of the evening. A man of few words, he *had* come to his only daughter's defense on one particular occasion. Her memory could not forget it.

Benjamin, during his allotted ten-minute stretch, had up and abandoned the butter churn for a quick cold drink at the well pump across the yard. Aware of his absence, Katie jumped to the task, taking her brother's turn and pushing the handle down . . . and up . . . then down again with all her might, though having an awful hard time of it.

Returning, Benjamin frowned, clearly put out. "Who said you could take my turn?"

Not to be denied her chance, she pressed on. No strength left to speak, Katie pushed deliberately with her little hands and arms, leaning into the motion as best she could.

"Katie!" hollered Ben, red-faced.

In an instant Dat was at her side, though she was so intent on the chore that she hadn't seen him get up from his spot on the lawn and hurry over. "Benjamin, you've *lost* your turn," Dat said flatly. "Katie and I will churn your ten minutes." And they did, and 'twas the end of the contest. 'Least for *that* night.

Smiling now, Katie found the memory amusing. Yet, the more her brain worked on it, the more she cherished the fact that Dat had taken her side against his son, his flesh-and-blood son, at that.

Dat loved me then, she thought, brushing a clump of dirt off a handsome medium-sized pumpkin and loading it onto a wheelbarrow.

———◆———

Before church on Sunday, as Katie dressed for the day, she talked over Eli's forthcoming wedding with her husband. "We can't expect to be invited, you know."

Dan nodded. "You're right about that. Still, I know this bothers you no end."

"Jah, 'tis something I must bear the rest of my life."

"Maybe not," Dan said, gathering her in his arms. "We'll trust the Lord to break the bonds of discord between our families."

Her darling was right, Katie knew. Still, the pain of rejection and separation plagued her night and day.

Then, lo and behold, if several women weren't chatting 'bout Eli's wedding at the meetinghouse. Seemed everyone knew 'bout the plans—the whereabouts and whatnot—but Katie herself. 'Course, some of the women were related, one way or another, to Eli's bride-to-be. Truth was, Katie had only met Grace Stoltzfus on one or two occasions at Sunday night singings—a good long time ago. Scarcely did she know the girl who was to become her own sister-in-law.

Taking her place on the left side of the church, along with the other women and children, she bowed her head in prayer. When it came time for the sermon, she thought the pastor's text—found in Luke's gospel—was surely for her.

No man, having put his hand to the plow, and looking back, is fit for the kingdom of God.

Attuning her heart to Jesus' words, peace began to fill her mind.

Up at daybreak, Katie sat at the kitchen table on Monday morning, drinking a hot cup of black coffee with Dan, looking out at the fields behind their house. The thing they liked most about this house was the way the small yard seemed to mingle, at the tree line, with the neighbor's cornfield. It gave the feeling of openness, of acres of land. She wondered if Dan ever missed farming alongside his father. Dan's father had wanted his son to follow in his boot prints; prob'ly still mourned the fact that Dan was off drafting building blueprints, pluckin' that evil guitar of his, and singing songs not found in the *Ausbund*—the sixteenth-century hymnal of the Amish church.

The sky was speckled with golden light as the sun rose over distant hills. Temperatures had surely fallen in the night; Katie could see the light frost that touched the trees and the remnants of her garden. Wouldn't be long till the creeks and ponds froze over and winter winds brought snow. For now, far as she could tell from Dan's *Farmer's Almanac*, another month of fairly mild autumn weather was in store for them. She was glad of that, as she was busy with fall canning, going from one house to another, helping her women friends put up hundreds of quarts of produce, laying in store for the winter.

She had, just this week, reconciled herself to Dat's rebuff, though she would abide the sting of separation from Amish loved ones. Just as her husband did. Dan, too, had not seen or conversed with his parents since the confession he'd offered at his father's knee, having met with solemn faces. His mother had cried when he kissed her cheek, bidding farewell. "My life is in God's hands," he'd told them, but neither had seen eye to eye with Dan. They did not accept his newfound faith, nor his Mennonite beliefs. A person who claimed salvation was a heretic, according to the Amish church. Assurance of salvation could not be had on this earth . . . not till the Judgment Day. To think or say otherwise was a display of arrogance, plain and simple. Yet his father had surprisingly accepted Dan's handshake that day. Katie and Dan couldn't expect much more than that, but they *could* pray for their parents' salvation. The least they could do was in effect the *most* they could do, believing in the power of prayer. So every day they joined hands, naming each of their relatives before the throne of grace.

Katie set down her coffee cup, stirring the coffee for no apparent reason. She recalled any number of early-morning breakfasts shared with her parents as a girl. Hearin' both the comical and not-so-funny tales Mamma liked to tell and re-tell—of near mishaps in the barn, unending mountains of dirty clothes, and all the peculiar and wonderful-gut things that happened over a lifetime of farm living. Young Katie always listened intently, ears wide open, enjoying the natural rhythm of her mother's storytelling voice, Dat nodding his head sometimes or putting in a word here or there, never spicing up the story, not one iota, just adding his particular view of the way things were.

Katie especially liked the story of Mamma's older brother's sixteenth birthday, when his father presented to him a racy black courting buggy, along with a spirited horse of his own. At his first Sunday night singing, Katie's Uncle Seth had spent much of the evening trying to catch the eye of "one 'specially perty girl," Mamma would say, an angelic grin on her face. The way the story went, Seth had bragged up and down to his wife-to-be—'cept she didn't know it at the time—'bout how his new buggy was better 'n all the others parked out in the barn-yard and just how fast his horse could run. "And wait'll you see how sharp I take 'em corners," he boasted.

Truth be told, the perty young girl wasn't impressed at all 'bout such nonsense. She was hoping for a serious young man to court her, someone who had sense enough to drive carefully *if* she agreed to be seen home by him. And she told him so! Stood right up to Uncle Seth the way no woman ever had, and that was the beginning of a three-year courtship that ended in marriage.

Katie thought back to her own *Rumschpringa*—her "running-around" years—and had to smile. Dan had used every excuse in the book to get her attention, long before she ever turned sixteen and started attending singings. Other fellas were interested, too, once she started showing up Sunday nights, and for a time she let several different boys take her home in their courting buggies. Dan spent one whole evening trying his best to line her up to ride home with him. After that, it didn't take long for them to settle into a somewhat secret courtship, the age-old custom amongst the People.

One frustrating yet funny night stood out in Katie's mind. Dan had been seein' her home for some months now, when on an exceptionally moonlit night several boys from the singing followed behind the courting buggy, unbeknownst to them. She and Dan had even stood next to the buggy for a while, talking softly to each other, holding hands, too.

When Dan tied up the buggy in the lane to walk Katie to her house, the boys made off with his horse. A gut trick, to be sure!

Just now, lookin' at her husband, Katie was sure something

was bothering him. Dan had been sitting too quietly, drinking his morning cup of coffee and staring out the window. Wasn't like him to think so awful hard at breakfast.

"Honey?" She reached across the table, touching his arm.

He looked at her thoughtfully. "Remember yesterday's sermon?" he asked.

She remembered, even recited the verse again, the one that rang in her memory. *Looking back, after finding your peace and beginning a work for the Lord, is fruitless.* The Bible said so.

"We must stop lookin' back," Dan said. "Hard as it may be."

She nodded, passing a platter of hot scrambled eggs and toast to him without saying a word, keeping her eyes on him.

He took the plate and dished up some breakfast. "I just don't see how I could ever turn my back on *my* son or daughter," he said.

"Tradition's got its hooks in our families. They need salvation, full and free." She knew he agreed wholeheartedly on the subject.

They held hands as Dan prayed a blessing over the breakfast and the day, his voice strong and confident. No doubt there'd be similar moments shared like this in the future. Katie knew they were growing in the Lord and in their love for each other. When one of them was down and hurting, the other was strong, and vice versa. That's just the way it had been since their courting days. And their love of music helped express their worship to the Creator-God who made them—sensitive and compassionate souls that they were. Made Katie wonder what on earth their future children might be like, having such similar parents.

While she was washing up the dishes, the phone rang. "Hullo," she said.

"How *are* ya, Katie?" It was Mamma.

"Oh, fine," she replied, hoping to hear of Eli's wedding plans.

"Haven't talked to you in the longest time, it seems."

"Where are you now?" She had to know—wanted to picture Mam's location.

"Remember the pay phone near the Bird-in-Hand Restaurant?"

Katie knew. "Everything all right?"

"Well . . ." Mamma paused for a second. "S'posin' you oughta hear the news from me, though you may've already heard of Eli's wedding to Grace Stoltzfus."

"Jah, I did . . . at church. Some of the women are second cousins to Gracie's mother, I guess."

Mamma sighed audibly. "Oh, Katie, I just hate the thought of you not bein' on hand to witness your brother's wedding vows, but—"

Katie's heart sank. "It's not for you to fret so. Dan and I will send over a wedding present in a few days." Then she added quickly, "We'll pray they have a long and happy life together."

"They do seem well matched, and Gracie isn't afraid of work a'tall. She cooks and bakes right alongside me; cans, too, with the other women in the district. Likes a good laugh— jokes, you know—just like Eli and Benjamin."

"They'll have plenty of time for seriousness, right?" Katie

laughed, making small talk, when what she really wanted was to get down to brass tacks. Just for once.

"Nice to hear your voice again, Katie. Everything all right there?" Mamma said *there* as if they were livin' clear on the other side of the world. But, in many ways, they surely were.

"We're fine." Then, thinking of her father, Katie asked, "How's Dat these days?"

" 'Bout the same" came the words.

Did he mention seeing me at the store? She dared not ask. Dared not look back after putting her hand to the plough. Yet the place reserved in her heart for her father was tender and bleeding, all the same.

"Write me another letter sometime," Katie said before their good-byes. "I love you, Mamma. You and Dat both." Honestly, she came close to saying "Tell him for me," but she kept her peace. Best this way.

◆

Dan said he was going for a walk . . . *before* going to the office? Well, it did seem a bit odd, but she said nothing and set about baking bread as she did each weekday morning.

Around eight o'clock Dan returned, comin' in the back door, his face bright, eyes wide. "I believe I know just what to do," he announced, "about reaching out to our families." He looked her square in the face. "Katie, it's time we move forward, past our shunning. If we can't go back to Hickory Hollow to our people, to witness, then we'll invite them here . . . to us."

The idea sounded good in theory, but unless God worked a miracle, there was no way either of their fathers would step foot in their house. For sure and for certain.

"What do you think of that?" He was asking for moral support. She saw it in his eyes.

"Have you prayed 'bout this?"

"I talked it over with the Lord just now, while I was walking." He smiled, lookin' ever so convinced. "I tend to think God dropped this into my heart."

"Then who am *I* to question?"

They went to prayer, 'bout inviting each set of parents to dinner, knowing the invitations would most likely be refused. At the outset, anyway. Just maybe—over time—if they kept askin', something might give.

"We can trust and pray," Katie said, feelin' as determined as the look on her dear husband's face. Thing was, they weren't just eager to renew family ties; they wanted to invite their loved ones into the *family of God*. More than anything.

"God sees our hearts," Dan said, kissing her good-bye before heading to work. "Let's stand back and watch the Lord work."

Katie had to smile. So full of faith was her darling, after having been deep in thought at the table earlier. " 'Stand still, and see the salvation of the Lord,' " she called after him.

Days came and went, and there was no response to the written invitations. Not from Dan's parents, not from hers.

Mamma, who Katie thought might have a chance to get away from the house and phone again—to politely refuse "on account of the shunning," but call just the same—did not.

Eli's wedding day was fast approaching. Mamma was prob'ly caught up with food preparations. Over two hundred people would likely gather for the ceremony and wedding feast at the Stoltzfus home. Katie planned to gather with some friends that morning—had to keep from thinking too hard 'bout missing her brother's special day.

Meanwhile, she made good use of their pumpkins, bakin' chiffon pies, pumpkin nut cookies, and pumpkin spice cake, taking them round to all her neighbors. "Sharing the bounty," like Mamma always said.

Once married and settled in their new home, Eli and Grace would be among those that Katie wanted to invite for dinner, as well. Whether Eli and his bride followed closely to shunning practices was their choice, of course, but she had a feeling—high hopes, really—that the younger generation might be more open to fellowship outside the Hickory Hollow church district. She thought of a number of family members to witness to over the next few months, one being Benjamin, her youngest brother and favorite. She and her husband would sow the seed of God's Word, if given the opportunity, then trust the Lord of the harvest to do as He saw fit.

Stand still, and see the salvation of the Lord. . . .

It was the morning of Eli's wedding, a bright dawn. Katie

was expected soon at the house of her dear friend, Darlene Frey, where three other women were gathering to make a big batch of apple butter. Enough to last through the winter.

But at the moment, Katie was surrounded by music staff paper, scattered all round her, some on the floor and more on the kitchen table. She'd gotten engrossed in trying to follow the rules of music notation. Important things that Dan had taught her. She was having a good time of it, creating a hymn of thanksgiving—a harvesttime theme—and was reluctant to leave her work behind.

Thoughts of Eli and Grace interfered, though, and she began putting away her music, then slipped into a sweater. In the car, Katie found herself looking at the sky, clear and blue. So happy, she was, for her brother and his new bride. God was surely shining down from on high. Mamma was usually the one voicing such comments 'bout the weather on a wedding day. Dat might nod his head and go along with her remarks, not one for makin' such statements, though.

If Katie hadn't been deep in thought, she would've turned right at the junction—to head to Darlene's house. Instead, she made a *left-hand* turn and found herself on the narrow two-lane stretch of road leading to Hickory Hollow.

Once on the dirt road, there was no turnin' back. 'Least not without stopping smack-dab in the middle and making a sharp turn, followed by repeated attempts to back up without driving into the ditch on either side. 'Course, she'd never made such a turnaround with a car, not here, but she could easily visualize what it might take to do such a thing. The road, if she stayed on it, would eventually take her past a familiar sandstone farmhouse, the house her father's ancestors had built over a hundred fifty years ago.

Not wanting to be seen in the area, she decided to pull off at a slightly wider shoulder in the road. It would be a mistake to run into any of the wedding party or have word spread that shunned Katie was snoopin' about the landscape. No, she couldn't let that happen. Not after the ruckus she'd caused at another wedding back when.

She was making an attempt at a sharp turn, when, in the rearview mirror, she spotted a bench wagon rumblin' down the lane behind her.

How strange, she thought, backing up. The horse-drawn cart always arrived the day *before* the wedding, bringing enough foldable wooden benches to accommodate a hundred people, give or take. Had so many folk promised to come that Eli had to call on another church district to help with more seating? She assumed that was the case.

Waiting for the horse and wagon to pass, she sat with her hands on the steering wheel. But just as the wagon came alongside her car, the horse stopped unexpectedly and reared up as if he was spooked. That's when she noticed the driver and passenger—Dat and Benjamin! Well, she hardly knew what to think.

Dat began pulling hard on the reins. And Ben jumped down, runnin' to the horse and grabbing the bridle, trying to calm him. By now a good many benches had already slid out the back of the wagon, falling down onto the dirt road.

Hurrying to alert Dat of the pickle he was in with the benches scattered behind, she didn't realize he hadn't seen her before, hadn't noticed that his daughter was the driver of the parked car, the car that prob'ly gave the horse such a fright.

Dat was wide-eyed when he spied her waving at him.

Ben hollered at her from where he stood with the horse. "Katie, what're *you* doing here?"

Thinking how awkward it would be to try 'n' explain that she'd made a wrong turn and wanted to make the U-turn in the road—but prob'ly couldn't—she ignored Ben's remark and looked at her father. "Some of the benches fell out the back of the wagon." She pointed toward them.

With a grunt, Dat climbed down, going round to see for himself.

Oh, it was ever so uncomfortable, her standing there while they worked, lifting the long, heavy benches back into the wagon. She didn't know whether to get in the car and drive off—and risk spooking the horse again—or just stay put. So she remained, wishing she could be of some help, yet knowing such a thing was out of the question. After all, the mishap was prob'ly her fault in the first place. If she'd gone the *other* way, toward Darlene's house, none of this would've happened. Today of all days.

She could just hear it now: "You'll never guess who we ran into this mornin'," Ben might say to one boy cousin or another. Jah, the news would spread like wildfire.

Humiliated, that's what she'd be. On top of bein' excommunicated and shunned, they would heap more shame on her.

Katie waited till all the benches were put back, till Benjamin and Dat got into the wagon yet again. Stood like a stiff statue, really, near holding her breath. Such an unbearable reunion this was.

Still, she waited for the wagon to move forward. But it

seemed to be parked there, lingering . . . for what reason she didn't know.

Suddenly, here came Dat down out of the wagon, walking toward the car. Toward *her*. He stopped 'bout an arm's length away, planted his feet just so in the dirt, head down for a second, then up came his eyes, catchin' hers. "God be with ya, daughter," he said, eyes glistening.

Daughter . . .

Katie hardly knew what to say. Then she did. "And with you," she replied.

Their eyes locked, but her father said no more. He turned to go, glancing back over his shoulder. He paused, then reached up and pulled himself into the wagon.

"'*Tis better to forgive than to hold a grudge.*" Dat's words, spoken long ago, came back to her again. And she felt nearly as light as the mockingbird flappin' short, rounded wings high overhead, its long-tailed shadow dipping here and there, through the reds and golds of autumn.

Long after the horse pulled the bench wagon on its way, the cart a-creakin' and swayin' toward a wedding ceremony— long after the cloud of dust settled a bit—Katie stepped back into her car. She was ready now to attempt the turn in the road. Jah, she would try.

The Telling

. . . as unto a light that shineth in a dark place,
until the day dawn, and the day star arise in your hearts.

—2 Peter 1:19

They'd spent nearly all day at their middle son's wedding, eating and talking with their extended family, having themselves a wonderful-gut time over at Gracie's parents' farm. Eli and his bride made a nice couple, they did, and Rebecca Lapp was right happy 'bout the match. Another daughter-in-law to sew and quilt with—cook and can with, too. And from what she knew of Gracie, well, this new addition to the family just might be an up-'n'-coming storyteller in the hollow.

As for Eli's marriage, movin' out of the house meant that son Benjamin, who would someday inherit the family farm, was the only one left to help shoulder the farming chores along with Samuel. And by the look of things—the pairing up of young couples that had gone on at Eli and Gracie's wedding dinner—well, Rebecca could only hope that Ben had found himself matched up with a nice girl for the day. Surely one of their own Plain girls would catch his eye, even though he'd

41

suffered heartache after bein' ditched by his longtime girlfriend last year. Rebecca had been cautious, hadn't questioned Ben 'bout the rumors flying round about a fancy English girl. If any of the tongue-waggin' was even true.

But Eli's wedding—and poor jilted Benjamin—weren't the only things on Rebecca's mind. Her thoughts were just a-churnin' as she stepped out of the carriage and made her way into the house while her husband unhitched Ol' Molasses and led the driving horse off to the barn. She thought hard 'bout the invitation that had come in the mail a while back . . . from their shunned daughter, Katie, of all things.

Seemed Katie and her Mennonite husband, Daniel Fisher, wanted to extend the hand of fellowship 'cross forbidden lines, inviting Samuel and her to dinner. *Call anytime*, Katie had written at the bottom of the note.

Rebecca *had* used a public pay phone now and then to make contact with her girl. Hadn't felt all too guilty 'bout doin' so, what with Bishop Beiler easing up some on one of the harshest shunnings in these parts. 'Course, she always used her time on the telephone wisely, mindful to nudge her daughter toward repentance and a quick return to her baptismal vow. Once or twice a month she talked to Katie. No more. Not like it oughta be with your one and only daughter, her bein' raised in an Old Order household and all. These years of Katie's young adulthood oughta be spent enjoyin' frequent quiltings and work frolics. Together with her mamma, talking face-to-face. But then, Rebecca believed her adopted daughter had been cut out of a different dye lot of life's fabric. Sure seemed so anyway.

———————◆———————

By the time Samuel came wanderin' into the kitchen, after hanging up his coat and dropping his for-gut shoes in the utility room, Rebecca had already set the table and put out a light supper of chicken salad and honey oatmeal bread for sandwiches, and white fruit salad made with unflavored gelatin, cold fruit juice, mayonnaise, whipping cream, icing sugar, pineapple slices, white cherries, and chopped nuts. She wanted to bring up Katie's invitation in the worst way, but she was sure Samuel wouldn't budge one little inch 'bout putting his feet under the table of a shunned—and Mennonite—son-in-law.

"Glad for an early supper," Samuel said, pulling out a chair to sit down. "Cows need milkin' soon."

Her husband's comment left things wide open for her to say something 'bout Benjamin, though she was fairly certain their youngest son wouldn't be home just now—nor anytime soon—on account of the late-night singing planned at the Stoltzfus home, expected after most every Amish wedding. "Did you get someone to help you in the barn, then?" she asked, steering clear of Benjamin for now.

"Jah, Bishop John's on his way over."

"*Our* bishop?" This was a surprise, indeed.

"Said he wouldn't mind helpin' out an old man."

She shook her head, sitting across from her husband now that their family had shrunk to almost nothing, 'specially those living at home anyways. "You ain't feeling so well today?" she asked, disregarding her husband's comment 'bout Bishop John's tactless remark.

"Ach, well enough." And with that, he bowed his head and silently prayed over the meal, and Rebecca joined him in doing so.

When the "amen" was said, she passed the chicken salad and bread to Samuel. "What made you think to ask the bishop for help with milkin'?"

He snorted gently. " 'Twas John's idea. Good of him, I should say."

Samuel wasn't one to mince words. The fact that John Beiler still held either of them in any regard was downright astonishing, as she thought on it. They'd purposely hid the truth of Katie's adoption from the People all those years, deceivin' nigh everyone in the hollow . . . before the Bann came on Katie, that is. Hardest thing Rebecca had ever endured.

She didn't mention it just now, but she guessed the bishop had something on his mind. Prob'ly why he was coming over 'fore too long. So, since her husband was thinking on the bishop's arrival, she decided against bringing up Katie's invitation. Somehow, it didn't seem quite right, seein' as how their daughter had refused to marry the widower-bishop one bright November day nearly two years ago now.

They ate in silence for the longest time. Then, clear out of the blue, Samuel looked up from his plate. "Saw Katie today." His words seemed to hang in the air.

"You did?"

He nodded, his beard touching his chest. "On the road, early this mornin'."

"Whatever was she doin' over in these parts on her brother's wedding day?"

Eyes serious, Samuel stared at his plate as if deep in thought.

"She wasn't on her way *here*, was she?" she pressed.

When he finally looked up, his jaw was clenched. "Seemed a bit lost, to tell you the truth."

"Well, how could that be?" Rebecca wondered what in the world Samuel was tryin' to say. Katie knew her way round Hickory Hollow, and she was a modern, car-driving Mennonite woman, too.

Scratching his head, he shifted in his chair. "Spoke to my daughter . . . first time since her shunning."

Rebecca daresn't allow a smile to shine on her face. No, that might spoil things. Besides, Samuel was nodding now, appearin' to be slightly pleased with himself. Maybe that he'd even told her. Then he reached for another piece of bread and nothing more was said of the encounter, though Rebecca wondered what had prompted him to share such news.

If nothin' else, this was a beginning. A new start, maybe. Yet she wouldn't get her hopes up too high. She'd wait a day or two and bring up the dinner invitation. See what Samuel made of it.

Rebecca couldn't seem to budge from her spot at the back door, lookin' out toward the barn. Curious as she was, she wouldn't think of going out there and interrupting whatever the two men were discussing just now. Surely Samuel wasn't telling the bishop 'bout his seein' Katie on the road today. No, she couldn't imagine *that* was being talked over. More than likely, John was talking blacksmithing duties and whatnot. Jah, that's prob'ly all. Though, she'd heard tell from the bishop's mother-in-law, Rachel Stoltzfus, that Mary had been feelin' *gnipplich*—sickly. "Under the weather," word had it. Rebecca wondered if Mary's marrying into a ready-made family, five youngsters and all, might not be taking its toll on the young woman.

She should've gone right over to visit Mary when she'd first heard of a problem. After all, Mary had been underfoot most all of Katie's growing-up years. Rebecca scarcely could recall a time when she and Katie were bakin' cookies or sweet-bread that Mary Stoltzfus wasn't right here in this kitchen, helping right along.

Thinking on it, she remembered just how busy things had been this past week, what with the food preparations for Eli's wedding falling squarely on her shoulders. *Hurting folk often get lost in the shuffle come wedding season*, she thought. Sad to say, but it was true.

So . . . she would make it a point to pay Mary a visit tomorrow.

◆

"Bishop John's concerned 'bout his wife," Samuel said, coming in from the barn.

"How's that?" she asked.

"Seems Mary's pining for . . . our Katie."

The girls had loved each other as sisters, sharing their childhood years so much that the People often thought of them as two peas in a pod, really. Why, they walked to school together every day, worked in each other's "charity" gardens, helped their mammas with chores, sewed for-gut dresses here, even baby-sat for neighbors together.

Samuel went on. "John asked if you might go see her."

"I'll drop everything tomorrow and go."

He went and sat in the hickory rocker in the corner of the kitchen. "Wouldn't be such a gut idea to invite Katie along, I'm thinking." A warning, true, but quite an unnecessary one, for she'd never thought of such a thing.

The whole Mary-'n'-Katie dilemma was a knotty problem. Both for Rebecca and her husband. "Such a sad and sorrowful thing when the shun is upheld at all costs." She surprised herself by blurting out the words, never much thinking how Samuel might take their meaning.

" 'Tis always much harder to turn one's back on 'thus saith the Lord' than on 'thus saith the church,' " came Samuel's sympathetic reply.

Rebecca wondered if his view on the shunning was weakening some. But she wouldn't presume to ask.

He rocked silently for a time. Then, slowly, he said, "I clearly see the purpose for social avoidance in the Scriptures, don't misunderstand. Sometimes, I just don't know if we oughta impose the Bann on folk who are wholly followin' the Lord—that is, if they prove themselves as being built up in the faith in their new church."

Well, now, she'd never heard Samuel talk *this* way. Thinking on his comment, she fell silent.

Rebecca waited till the bishop's children had gone to school the next day before setting off toward the peaceful spread of land. She was glad for a morning all to herself. This way she could reflect on her and Samuel's further discussion last evening. Seemed all he wanted to talk 'bout was Katie and the peculiar situation they, as a family, found themselves in. At first she'd thought him a bit peeved at her, but he had been tryin' his best to be understood. For the first time in many months, he'd opened up his heart to her. In the end, after a gut long time of it, they'd come to grips with the shunning quandary, its divisive overtones. And since they were deep in such talk, she'd stuck her neck out and shared with Samuel the invitation that had come in the mail from Daniel and Katie.

Samuel had visibly bristled, but as they talked, he seemed slightly open to having Katie, at least, come over to *their* house for a short visit. But not the other way round. "And not for a meal, mind you." He'd added quickly, " 'With such an one no not to eat,' according to First Corinthians."

Shunning a former church member—daughter or no—had a way of disrupting close-knit families. Couldn't help but. As for the years stretching out ahead, Rebecca could only think that Samuel's dairy-farming days were coming to an end and prob'ly here perty quick. If Benjamin *did* marry come next year, they had just twelve months or so to work through all the aspects of their youngest son takin' over the farm and their moving into the vacant Dawdi Haus connected to their rambling farmhouse. Goodness knows, forty-five acres was a lot of land for one man and his son to keep up Old Order style, including draft mules, driving horses, and dairy cattle.

'Course, *she* wouldn't mind slowin' down some. She just might be ready to give up their side of the big house soon, let Benjamin and his young wife—and a growing family—take over the reins of farming life.

She thought of assuming the quiet yet strong matriarchal role of the Lapp family. Her own mother had blessed her and Samuel's days, and their children's, by living in the addition with Rebecca's ailing father for a gut many years. Maybe 'twouldn't be so bad moving over there, after all.

Yet she sensed what was causin' her to suffer so. Had nothing to do with growing older or retiring from farm chores, really. Had much more to do with the loss of her daughter, not knowing what the future held. And Dan, too, who was a big part of Katie's life now. What *would* become of her and Katie's close relationship? What would happen when Katie's little ones started coming along, Rebecca being their grandmammi and not spending much time with them? What then?

Lamenting such things, she knew full well how dear Mary must be feeling these days, living her life cut off from Katie, recallin' all the fond memories, the happy days—sensing Katie just round the corner, which truly she was, yet having no contact. No good fellowship with a lifelong best friend. My, oh my, how could it be?

Rebecca's heart was heavy as she walked down Hickory

Lane under the spotlight of the sun, amidst a blaze of red sugar maples and sumacs. As she neared Bishop John's place, marked by three mulberry trees, she hoped she might bring cheer to Mary despite her own dismal outlook.

◆

Rebecca found Mary busy baking orange nut bread when she arrived. The familiar tangy aroma filled the kitchen, and she quickly hung her shawl on a peg in the utility room, asking if there was anything she could do to help.

According to Mary the housework seemed to be "all caught up," and she invited Rebecca to sit down while coffee was poured. "Oh," Mary said, catching herself. "I guess I oughta ask if you'd rather have some tea?"

"No . . . no. Coffee's just fine," she replied, noticing Mary's hollow eyes and drawn face.

Once they started talking there was no stopping either of them. Mary wanted to chat 'bout her life with the bishop. "Most folk don't have any idea, but there's such a burden on a minister," she said solemnly. "And a wife tends to bear it right along with him."

Rebecca didn't know firsthand, but she'd heard enough 'bout the sorrow of bein' a leader over the People that it was surely a sober responsibility, overseeing the church community thataway. "A bishop's wife needs encouragement, I'm sure." She thought for a moment. "Does John often share the burden with you?"

Mary nodded, then frowned. "Not much. Sometimes I wish he would share more."

They talked a gut half hour or more, then Mary began telling Rebecca how she lies next to John at night, her heart breaking nearly in two sometimes when she hears the bishop's deep sighs, taking the needs of the People ever so seriously. "Not always, but sometimes in the morning, his pillow is damp with tears, so I put it in front of the wood stove to dry."

Rebecca found herself glancing toward the stove for the bed pillow, but there was none this day. "How are *you* doing, Mary?" she asked.

Mary forced a smile. "If you mean, am I happy as John's wife, jah, I am."

"Well, now, it's right nice seeing the love between the two of you . . . but how are you *feeling* these days?"

That opened the floodgates again for poor Mary, who broke down when she told of wanting to be a good mamma for John's children, but struggling some days, tryin' her best to meet the needs of everyone in the house.

"That's what a gut wife and mother does," Rebecca said. "A gut bishop, too—for the People. But sometimes things catch up with a person. There's more to life than busyness. Rest is important . . . and a gut book now and then." She hoped she was helping, by what she said. "It takes some doing, pacing oneself."

"I just seem to keep pushing myself here lately," Mary confessed.

"Well, why don't I come over a couple afternoons a week for a while, let you spend some time by yourself while I cook supper . . . be there for the children after school and whatnot."

"Would ya?" Mary brightened.

Rebecca nodded. "You're the type of woman who always sees things to do. I know, I'm the same way. And Katie's a lot like that. . . ." She stopped herself. Hadn't wanted to bring up her daughter. Not today.

Mary's eyes widened. "Oh . . . how *is* Katie?"

Sighing, Rebecca pushed ahead. "She and Daniel seem happy as larks. They've found a ministry Katie says they're both 'called to.' Mennonites have a different view on church music, ya know."

Mary seemed to understand. "Next time you see Katie, will ya tell her I pray for her every day . . . that she'll come to repentance?"

Rebecca didn't know what to say to that. Truth was, Katie and Dan seemed content to "serve the Lord" in their new church. She wondered if the time might come when her "saved" daughter and son-in-law returned to the Amish church, but she was hesitant to say much more to Mary, who seemed so eager that it might be so.

"Next time I talk to her, I'll tell her what you said."

Mary fell silent, gripping her coffee cup too tight, it seemed. Then she added, "I miss Katie more than I can say. Would love to see her again."

Lest words fail her and both women end up grieving outwardly, Rebecca said no more.

"Haven't found such a dear friend as Katie in any of John's sisters, and no girl cousin comes even close," Mary continued.

Sitting there in the quietude of Mary's big kitchen, the beauty of the fields stretching out to the sky outside the window, Rebecca thought 'twas the saddest thing she had witnessed of late, this misery on Mary's face. "We must remember that it was Katie who left *us* . . . she's the one who broke her baptismal vow to God and the church," Rebecca said.

"I never thought she would show such discontentment," whispered Mary, weeping softly.

Reaching out to the young woman, she touched Mary's hand. Surely the bishop's wife was dwelling on the problem of Katie and Dan's car ownership and them playin' their guitars hither and yon—that they'd forced the People's hand by embracing the world and all it had to offer. Had they merely gone off to another church, the chances of lifting the shun might've been something of a consideration. But owning and driving a car, embracing electricity and music—and breaking their baptismal vow—that was the biggest problem. Such action confirmed a restless spirit, one seeking after worldly things.

"Maybe you and Gracie—Eli's wife—will become close friends," Rebecca said.

That brought a smile to Mary's face. "Invite her over sometime, jah?"

Rebecca agreed. "I hear Gracie's got a nice way with a story."

"There's only *one* storyteller in the hollow." Mary squeezed Rebecca's hand. "We all know who that is."

"Well, this here Teller ain't getting any younger. There's always room for another, I daresay." Then, thinking on it, Rebecca had an idea. "Let me tell you a true story right now," she said softly. "Maybe this'll help some."

Mary blew her nose and listened, the lines in her brow softening a bit as Rebecca began to describe a close relationship between identical twin sisters, "who lived in Somerset

County in the Laurel Highlands of the southern Allegheny Mountains—where the big thing is to churn butter by hand. 'Course, there were other festivals, too, like the Maple Festival in April and other craft-related ones at other times during the year.

"Well, these girls grew up sharing nearly everything—the same bedroom and hobbies, going to singings and hoedowns, attending quiltings and work frolics. Never, ever apart.

"Along 'bout the time when Fannie and Edna started taking their baptismal classes so they could join church come fall, Edna met a young man outside her church district and began spending time with this New Order Amish fella named Perry Mast. 'Course, the friendship caused a rift between the twins— the first ever—along with a big stir in the community. Truth be known, Perry, a best friend of Edna's Mennonite cousin, loved Edna and was bound and determined to take her as his wife, even after both Fannie and Edna bowed their knees before the bishop and were baptized 'before God and these many witnesses.'

"Even when Fannie begged Edna not to marry Perry— 'Won'tcha find a nice Amish boy?' she pleaded—Edna ran off and married him anyway. But then, that wasn't the worst of it. Any sin, no matter how small, must be dealt with if it causes disharmony amongst the People. So her parents and the preachers called on Edna and asked her to confess her sin to the Lord and make gut on her promise to God and the church, but she would not return to her Amish community. Yet again, one of the preachers approached her 'bout her leaving her vow behind. And her parents pleaded and cajoled her.

" 'Course, by now, Perry, her husband, was starting to get a bit peeved, all these folks comin' over, saying his bride was a sinner and all."

Mary stirred a bit. "What happened then?" she asked.

"The membership voted to shun Edna. Said she could never have anything to do with her twin sister again. 'Not in this life, and only in the life hereafter, if you will but confess your sins and repent' was the warning given.

"One year passed, then another, and both Fannie and Edna became sick with grief, suffering so that Edna had to see a doctor, who said she needed a good dose of visiting. 'That's all that's wrong with you,' he said. 'You're homesick for your family.' "

Mary looked a bit worried. "What did the sisters do . . . surely they didn't disobey the shun?"

"Didn't dare do that, 'cause Fannie was afraid of the Bann falling hard on her next thing. So the girls arranged for a mutual friend, a go-between, to visit one and then the other, delivering messages. That didn't suffice, though, and it wasn't long before Edna developed a crippling form of arthritis and she and her new family moved away from Pennsylvania."

"Where'd she go?"

"Last I heard, somewhere in Arizona."

Mary's eyes were wide. "Did they ever see each other again?"

Rebecca was sorry, but she had to shake her head. "Such a sad story 'tis, the tearing apart of beloved sisters, all due to disobedience."

"Sin has its way of separating," Mary said. "I know that all too well."

"Fannie, far as I know, hasn't stopped praying for Edna to come to her senses."

"Then . . . they're still living?" Mary asked.

"Nigh unto their mid-seventies now."

"Are they relation to you?"

Not wanting to reveal just how close a kinship Fannie and Edna were, all Rebecca said was, "They're some of Samuel's cousins."

It was Mary's turn to wonder. "Does Katie know this story?"

"Many a time, I told it when she was little. So my daughter knows it well, and if she listened—and I 'spect she did—she surely understands 'bout the freedom to return, to ask forgiveness."

Mary folded her hands reverently. "I don't see how our Katie could go and do near the same thing as Edna." She sighed audibly. "I just don't see how. . . ."

Rebecca hadn't told the story to upset Mary further. No, but now that she looked into Mary's face, she could see there was a glimmer of hope. The young woman had taken the story to heart. There were others who'd walked the agonizing road Mary now trod, yet they hadn't lost heart, trusting the Lord God heavenly Father for grace and mercy.

"You're not alone in your grief, Mary. We'll keep remembering our loved ones in prayer, each and ev'ry one." Pausing, Rebecca looked out at the trees shedding their autumn finery, depositing crisp heaps of red and orange leaves on the ground below. " 'Tis not our place to try 'n' force an erring one home," she said finally, reaching for her coffee cup.

Mary got up quickly. "Here, let me pour you some more."

"*Denki*—thank you, Mary," was all Rebecca could say just now. The Telling had taken ever so much out of her. Far more than she'd expected.

———————◆———————

Rebecca assured Samuel that Mary seemed to be doing all right. She didn't tell everything that had been said between the two women. Not that Mary had asked for her confidence, 'twasn't that. She just felt the things Mary had shared about the bishop—his heavy burden for the People—wasn't something to bring up just now. "Mary needs a close friend, someone to take Katie's place until . . ." She couldn't finish. Too painful, it was.

Samuel pushed up his glasses. "Well, now, I wouldn't be looking for Katie to confess anytime soon; Dan neither. Prob'ly won't at all."

She eyed her husband, this man who was known to follow every jot and tittle of the *Ordnung*. She shouldn't have been too surprised at his statement. "Once electric gets its grip on a person, well . . . and automobiles, too. Jah, you're prob'ly right," she agreed.

"There's much more to it than flirting with modern ways." He was close to making a point. She could see it in the way he set his jaw, put down his paper, and began rockin' in the chair to beat the band. "I've seen it time and again—folk who leave the church only to claim they have salvation. They don't usually return to the Old Ways. If they profess that their sins have been forgiven and they're on their way to heaven . . .

well, I'd say they won't be kneeling before the membership in repentance."

"Why *is* that, do ya think?" Honestly, Rebecca wanted to know how the "assurance of salvation" doctrine taught in certain groups could seize a person, so as to confuse their minds. The Old Order believed in the *hope* of salvation, as taught in the book of Ephesians.

"Between you and me, I've been reading parts of the New Testament, tryin' to see just what it is Katie's got that's so different from how she was raised. All I can say is 'Strait is the gate, and narrow is the way, which leadeth unto life, and few there be that find it.' "

Rebecca took that to heart. Samuel *did* believe their church was the one and only. Yet, Katie had openly shared the life-changing experience that had "set her free," as she put it. Right convincing, it was. Her daughter had declared that peace wasn't found in doing good works, not even in following Old Order rules, but in giving your heart wholly unto the Lord Jesus, accepting God's "gift of salvation." Sounded simple enough, if true. Yet, why did Samuel fight it so?

Samuel rose from his chair. "If they'd just stayed away from the music . . . and the car." He said it softly, maybe hoping not to be heard.

Sadly, she watched her husband hobble through the kitchen toward the front room, where he fell into the chair nearest the window. Prob'ly staring out at the splendor of leaves and sky, ever grateful for a bountiful harvest and a time of rest for the land and its caretakers.

On another day she would raise the issue of Benjamin's future here as a farmer. Maybe it'd be best told in story form—

a young man finds and marries a Plain girl and settles into the elder parents' house, them moving over to the Dawdi Haus.

Looking in on Samuel, his eyelids a-drooping now, she let him be. While he snoozed in the sunshine, she would drive horse and carriage to a telephone somewhere, give her Katie a call. After that, she might stop in to see how Eli and Gracie were getting along. Time she got better acquainted with her new daughter-in-law, storyteller 'n' all. Time she encouraged Gracie to pay a visit to the bishop's lonely wife. Jah, she'd do that today. This fine autumn afternoon in Hickory Hollow.

Down Hickory Lane

A little work, a little play,
To keep us going—and so, good day!
—Daphne du Maurier

Her late husband had always said a body oughta smell like dirt at the end of a spring day. Well, here it was well into autumn, and Ella Mae smelled so strong of the soil she wouldn't be waiting till Saturday night for a bath.

Against her doctor's orders, she'd spent part of the afternoon digging round in her flower garden, pulling up dried-up stems, planning ahead for next spring. 'Course, her Dutch hyacinth bulbs would be sprouting to life come next April, and she looked forward to the star-shaped, fragrant florets, brilliant in blues and pinks. And her rock garden—well, she had big plans for that next spring and summer. Sometimes she felt like an artist when it came to coordinating her plants and flowers, lettin' her imagination guide her, "painting" her canvas of soil and rock.

For now, though, she enjoyed watching her great-grandchildren play in the leaves piled up in the yard and over near the barn, where the wind kept a-shovin' them in unpredictable bunches. Seemed to her, adults were the only ones who ever thought of the extra work the fall months required, raking leaves and disposing of them, and whatnot all.

But children ... now, they were a different story. Even though the youngsters were s'posed to be out there raking, more often than not she'd see them spinning round like tops, making themselves dizzy, then falling into the knee-deep piles. Ach, so much fun they were having. Made her recall her own childhood. Sitting there in her rocking chair, the Wise Woman let her mind wander back a *gut* many years. . . .

"Work's fun, ain't so?" Mamma liked to say.

Young Ella Mae, on the other hand, preferred board games or books to helping out round the house. Wasn't till Mamma introduced her to baking, which included sampling the batter and dough and, of course, eatin' some of the final product— sweet oatmeal-and-raisin cookies or chocolate-chip bars—that Ella Mae decided work *was* fun. 'Least baking was.

Mam was smart thataway. There were times when she enticed her daughters to redd up the bedrooms, changing sheets and dusting, with the promise of chicken and dumplings for lunch. "The sooner we finish cleanin', the quicker we'll eat." Mamma's gentle, persuasive prodding taught them by example that work was, indeed, fun.

So whether Ella Mae washed the dishes or hoed the garden, work was play, 'specially when shared with Essie, her twin sister. A happy home was a place where work represented the love shared.

Once her baby brothers and sisters came along, there was

even more joy to be had. Each day they were reminded of the benefits of hard work. And Mamma was always on hand to help turn choring into a game.

The hardest summer of her life started after school ended in late spring the year she was eleven. Ella Mae had been sent off to work the whole summer for her grandparents at their farm. She secretly resented the arrangement, though she had nothing to say 'bout any of it. For her, the worst thing about working hours and hours every day in the hot sun, picking beans or strawberries, or whatever Mammi said to do, was knowing that sister Essie was back at home helping Mamma, while *she* was helping her aging grandparents, instead of the other way round.

Next summer, Essie and I will trade places, Ella Mae thought, hoping it would be so.

Early one evening, after shelling peas till her fingertips were nigh unto purple, she went for a walk down the main road, which by now she knew by heart. Perhaps it was the sun-filtered haze over the cornfields, the long road spilling out before her, or maybe the gnawing, aching tiredness in her arms and legs, she didn't know, but she was terribly homesick and considered writing Mamma a letter to tell her so. 'Course, she wouldn't say all the pent-up things in her mind just now. Wouldn't let her emotions run away with her. Truth was, she was madder 'n a hornet 'bout being shuffled off away from home at such a tender age. Seemed heartless, almost.

On either side of the road, whitewashed fences and farmhouses, bee-buzzin' apple orchards, and boundless fields of freshly planted corn lay unchanged after decades. Her people had settled here hundreds of years before, many of them buying up large parcels of land, constructing first the barns, then the houses. A lone cow, shaded by a sycamore tree, watched her blankly, uncaringly as she passed.

Then suddenly, a car crept up on her. Out of nowhere it seemed to come, hardly making a sound. Had she been oblivious to her surroundings, too deep in thought for her own good?

"Say, there, young girl!" someone called to her.

She made the mistake of lookin' to see who it was. And when she did, she caught sight of a black camera, out the car window, aiming its lens straight at her.

In the wink of an eye, she turned away. Wasn't gonna be caught unawares. These were surely English tourists out looking for an unsuspecting soul to capture on film. Well, she was smarter than to let something like *that* happen to her.

So she began to run, fast as her aching legs could manage, makin' a beeline toward a red-brick house covered on one side in blue wisteria vines. The farmhouse, turned out, belonged to an Old Order Mennonite farmer and his wife. Cheerfully, they took her in, offering milk and sugar cookies, warm from the oven. She told what had just happened out on the road. "The Englischers nearly had me in their camera," she said, still breathless.

"Well, we're just glad you thought to come running here to us," said the farmer's wife.

"Hate to think what Mamma would say just now," she blurted out before ever thinking.

The missus had the kindest blue eyes. "Aw, now, don't go worryin' yourself. Ain't your fault what happened."

She wondered at the time how the Lord God heavenly

Father might size up the situation. After all, the Old Testament law 'bout not making any graven image had come straight from God in the first place. So why had He allowed those tourists to make her sin thataway?

Just then she thought better of writing home to Mamma to complain 'bout being "farmed out." Instead, she would ask Mamma this very question. See what *she* thought.

Meanwhile, Ella Mae had stumbled upon some new friends, discovering the neighbors had the dearest little boys—six of 'em all in a row—'cause their mamma wanted a daughter in the worst way. After two boys, they'd had a set of twins and then another set of twins—all boys. Ella Mae wondered if she wasn't a glad sight. *That's why they like me*, she decided. *I'm a girl!*

When she returned to her grandparents' house, she told Mammi what had happened. "One gut thing 'bout it," she said, "I met the neighbors down the road apiece . . . and they invited me to visit anytime."

Mammi assured her that they were God-fearin' folk, and Ella Mae could go whenever her chores were caught up. Turned out the Mennonite farmers made work as much fun as Mamma always had, and Ella Mae spent many pleasant evenings over there helping with the boys, even baby-sat some off 'n' on that summer for a little rare pocket change.

When a letter from Mamma did arrive in the mail, Ella Mae tore it open with all eagerness.

My dear Ella Mae,

It was so nice to hear from you. I'm glad you're doing all right there. We all look forward to summer's end and seeing you again. Meanwhile, be a sweet girl and help Mammi and Dawdi all you can.

As for the Englischers and that camera of theirs, you mustn't worry that you did any sinning. On the contrary, really. I don't know how many tourists I've run into, even as a grown woman, who are picture-happy. It's their fault, not mine. My, my, they just don't seem to have any manners, pointing cameras at Plain folk. Now, you mustn't fret over such a thing. God's love continues to shine down on you. Remember that always.

Essie says "hullo" just now as I'm writing. She's ever so busy here, helping me with the younger children, cleaning and cooking, and often goes out with Dat, working the mules in the field.

We miss you, but trust the good Lord to take care of you while we're absent one from the other.

> *Love,*
> *Mam*

Ella Mae set the letter aside on the bureau to read again later, before bedtime.

Essie's workin' the mules with Dat, she thought. *Poor girl.*

Well, now, maybe helping out here wasn't so bad, after all. Worst thing she could think of was working one row after another, the boiling sun scorching you near to death. 'Least with picking or preparin' produce, a body could get out of the sun now and then, slip under a shade tree . . . drink a nice tall glass of cold lemonade.

Jah, 'twas good of Mam to write. Yet seeing the familiar handwriting stirred up the homesickness even more. Fighting back tears, she headed downstairs for evening prayers.

At breakfast the next morning, Mammi lined out the activities of the day. "We'll weed all the flower beds . . . the marigolds in the window boxes, too."

Ella Mae was glad to hear it, ready for a change of pace.
Gardening was lots more fun than picking strawberries or
shelling peas. But she would work hard, earn her keep and
then some for Dawdi to send home to her parents.

She sensed that something had changed in her. She felt
wonderful-gut, knowin' she was truly helping her family by
staying the summer long. And being cheerful 'bout it helped
her.

Seemed that's how it was during all the rest of July and
August, her settlin' into a routine of hard work on the farm,
occasional baby-sitting for the Mennonite children down the
road, long nights of rest for her weary body, church attendance
on Sunday, and twice, a visit from Mamma, Dat, and the family. After their first visit, she decided it wasn't such a bad
thing, them comin' to see her and then leaving, not takin' her
home just yet. 'Twasn't nearly so hard as she thought, actually
took the edge off her homesickness.

Come the second visit, well, summer's toil was nearly past.
School would be starting and she'd be going home. . . .

Ella Mae moved away from the window, glancing at the
day clock over her kitchen stove. Wouldn't be but a minute
and her great-grandchildren would come a-scurrying inside,
eager for an afternoon snack. She'd give 'em homemade cookies from the big apple-shaped jar on the counter, maybe slip
some chocolate syrup into their tall glasses of milk. Jah, today
she would spoil them just a bit—hardworkin' wee souls, they

were. Make a fuss over the children, whose faces were tender and true, who looked you straight in the eye when they talked, whose little features bore the semblance and down-to-earth honesty of their parents and their parents' kin before them.

She thought, *My, oh my, wouldn't my husband be mighty pleased—if he were alive today—our great-grandyoung'uns raking them leaves, tidying the place up. Dirt under their fingernails.*

Smiling, she opened the back door, welcoming the laughter of her grandchildren's offspring and the changing of the seasons both, her hands still a-reekin' of God's green earth.

Benjamin

Rejoice, O young man, in thy youth; and let thy heart cheer thee in the days of thy youth, and walk in the ways of thine heart, and in the sight of thine eyes: but know thou, that for all these things God will bring thee into judgment.

—*Ecclesiastes 11:9*

Awakening to darkness, Katie, in a dreamy stupor, thought surely she was back in her bedroom at Hickory Hollow, that it was time to "rise 'n' shine," hurry into choring clothes, get out to the barn to help with the milking. But as she lay there listening, ears attuned for her father's call up the steps, she realized she was no longer a girl growing up in the Lapp home. She was a young married woman, curled up next to Dan, her sleeping husband.

Morning's pale light had not seeped under the bedroom curtains, where cotton fabric gently brushed against the windowsill. Not a sound was heard, not even the first *peep-peepings* of a family of birds who'd camped out in the maple tree just yards from their window, birds who'd waited longer than usual to fly south. This being market day, a number of horse-drawn buggies would surely be passing by the house, yet the road was still as night.

Must be nearly dawn, Katie thought, too weary to raise herself and peer over the blanketed mound that was her husband to see the exact time on the illuminated alarm clock.

Lying in the stillness, her drowsiness slowly lifting, she thought of Mam, who'd called the other day, sharing news of a recent visit with Mary Beiler. "She misses ya something awful, Katie. We *all* do." Mam sounded a bit sad and recounted her morning over at the Beiler home. "Mary's got her hands full with John's children, no question 'bout that."

"They're *her* children now, too," Katie had said, hoping her friend had fallen in love by now with the red-cheeked youngsters.

"Jah . . . but can you just imagine?" Mamma hadn't said much more, prob'ly catching herself, realizing that Katie, too, had cared deeply for the Beiler brood—three boys and two girls—having nearly become their stepmamma a while back.

"Is the youngest, Jacob, in first grade yet?" Katie had been especially fond of the bishop's mischievous blue-eyed boy.

"Jah, and he works so hard at school . . . Mary tells me."

Hearing Mam talk up so 'bout Mary's stepchildren seemed ever so awkward. "That's not to say Jacob isn't *schmaert*—smart, really. Just got himself an active mind . . . awful hard to keep his attention on book learnin' when he'd prob'ly rather be outside catching a frog down by the creek, you know."

They chatted about several upcoming quiltings, though Mam wasn't the one to bring up the subject. Katie had asked about one frolic after another. Seemed there were several more round the corner, too, and Mam, when pressed for more information, said she would be helpin' her daughters-in-law, Annie and Gracie, put up preserves and vegetables for the long winter.

Perking up her ears at the mention of Annie Fisher, Dan's sister, Katie said, "Oh, and how *is* Annie . . . little Daniel, too?" Katie hadn't seen her oldest brother's wife and baby in ever such a long time.

Mam chuckled a bit. "Well, Daniel's growin' up fast, not much of a baby anymore. He's nearly two and all mixed up on his sleep schedule. Doesn't seem much interested in napping here lately . . . puts the *g* in go, I should say. Annie says he's been getting up in the middle of the night, just a-wailing. Must be he's cutting his second molars."

Katie could hardly believe her ears. Elam and Annie's baby a toddler? Where had the time gone?

Mam asked how she and Daniel were getting along, and Katie caught her up a bit on their lives, telling of one church function after another, of Dan's and her playing their guitars at small home groups, and her weekly visits to shut-ins with another friend, Darlene Frey. She told Mam that Darlene lived not far from Hickory Hollow—to the east a bit—and that they'd had such "good fellowship" here lately. She didn't go too far with that, though. Didn't say just how close she felt to Darlene these days, them both seein' eye to eye on certain Scriptures and all.

Later in the conversation, Mam suggested Katie "drop by for a chat sometime," saying that Dat was agreeable to it, but only if the visit was kept short. Mamma's faltering manner made Katie wonder if her mother was hesitant about a face-to-face meeting. And, too, it was clear that Dan wasn't invited. Not a'tall.

Katie, of course, didn't promise anything definite, saying she didn't know how soon she could visit them. She would talk things over with Dan first, wanted to get his opinion on the matter, whether or not he thought Katie oughta be singled out. Not that she was too timid to go alone, wasn't that. Dan just might think her parents were working on her, trying to get her "to see the light," according to the Old Ways.

Practicing hymns and gospel songs on their guitars, then leading worship at two different home groups during the past week had taken up much of her and Dan's time, so she hadn't shared Mam's phone call with him. But she would.

For now she plumped her pillow and lay quietly. Then, gently, she reached over and laid her hand on his shoulder, waiting for dawn's light . . . and for the alarm clock. So strong was Dan, both physically and in the faith. She could lean on him if need be when things troubled her. He was her shelter in the one and only howling gale of her life, because he fully understood the pain of shunning. Dan was under the Bann, too, from the same bishop, the man she'd nearly married. How strange that her dearest friend, Mary, had become John Beiler's young bride. Well, she was right happy for them both. Truly, she was.

Still, she couldn't help but wonder if Mary would go on missing her and telling Mamma so, who in turn would relay the information to Katie. Was it an attempt to get to Katie, make her feel sorrowful for leaving? To make her regret abandoning her Amish roots for her newfound faith?

Sitting up, she pushed back the covers, swinging her legs

over the side of the bed. Her feet groped about for slippers, and, finding them, she tiptoed across the room. At the window, she stood silently and parted the curtains, looking out. The dawn was as cold and gray as any she'd witnessed lately. An enormous cloud mass hovered over the horizon, blocking out the sun. No wonder the room had seemed so dark upon her first awakening.

She stared down at black tree trunks, mere etchings against a yellowing, now-dormant front lawn. In the distance, not a flicker of sunlight escaped from the gloom as the day began over wooded hills.

During breakfast Katie thought of telling Dan of her phone chat with Mam. But she was reluctant to do so. She couldn't bring herself to tell her beloved that Mamma wasn't much interested in including *him* in the invitation. So she decided to let it be, put off mentioning anything this morning. Instead, she would pray for the right timing. No need hurting her darling, who sat across the table, looking cheerful in his bathrobe, blond hair disheveled a bit, enjoying his bacon and eggs, glancing every so often outside at the drizzle coming from mournful skies. No, this could wait.

After Dan left the house for work, she spent the morning redding up the front room, a sunny living space, not large but ample enough for entertaining several couples at a time. Wiping down the white wall paneling, she paid special attention to the section that ran up alongside the stairway, where handprints seemed to show up most often. That done, she moved the brown wicker chests off the wide landing below and damp-mopped the hardwood flooring, checking in the corners for dust bunnies, as she'd heard them called as a teenager, when she used to clean house for English folk.

She smiled at the memory of a story she'd heard of a young boy who'd learned in church that all of us come from dust and will return to dust. At home he peered beneath his bed and said, "Well, someone's either coming or going under my bed!"

Standing back, she took in the informal room, its garden-like cane table and sofa blending easily with the oak pressed-back chairs, the sheer lace curtains—nothing at all like the Amish-green window shades of her upbringing—and plentiful potted plants. An old workbench, cut down and stained dark by Dan, doubled as their coffee table, creating a casual country look. They'd placed the beautiful corner cupboard, made by Dat, in one nook nearest the dining room. There she show-cased her prettiest china, especially teacups and saucers, and dainty glass salt-and-pepper shakers.

Moving to the wide bay window, she stared out, watching two squirrels chase each other across the front yard. "Thank you, Lord, for this day," she prayed. "Please bless my husband as he works, and touch the hearts of my Amish family. . . . Help me find the way back to Dat's heart. Amen."

The house seemed somehow too quiet just then, so she went to the kitchen and turned on the radio. Her favorite Christian station was airing an old hymn. On such a gray-weather day, the music filled the house with warmth and joy. Then, as the song ended and the announcer came on, the comment was made as to the importance of "putting feet on prayer." This wasn't the first time she'd heard it said. Mammi Essie, her maternal grandmother, often spoke of not just assisting strangers in need but reaching out to "help our own," she'd often say. The mutual aid society was a big part of Amish culture, and the philosophy continued to affect both her and Dan in their new church community, as well. She recalled here recently that a young Plain couple had lost their home to fire, including their furnishings, heirloom quilts, and china, along with their wedding gifts, too. But the women—aunts, cousins, and neighbor friends—rallied round and began making new quilts, sewing new clothes. Some of the men helped by contacting a builder who was sympathetic to the People, putting different folk in touch with one another, and soon blueprints were drawn up and subcontractors signed on . . . till a new house was erected.

She got to thinking of Mary and the bishop's children as she turned her attention to cooking up a pot of vegetable soup. What if she made some extra, froze it, and dropped it by Mary's in a few days? Surely a gesture like that wouldn't be misunderstood. Surely not. She'd thought of doing this very thing many times over the past months. Yet not wanting to stir up a commotion in the hollow, she'd thought better of it, keeping to herself and her husband, their church friends and acquaintances. Still, the radio announcer's words had struck a chord in her, and she decided to take the chance of her soup bein' rejected. Herself too.

After all, Mary had been her benchmark, so to speak. Mary made her laugh. And they'd cried together many a time. She could easily talk over anything with her closest friend, from the biggest problems to the smallest. Everything in life that was dear to her—all the important events—had always been shared with Mary.

What now? Was she to assume that Mary's marriage to the bishop would relegate her friend to the exclusive life of the Old Order forever? Was she to think that Mary's stand against salvation through grace was sufficient enough to keep Katie from "putting feet to prayer"?

Well, if ever there was a time to show the love of the heavenly Father, it was now. Katie set about cooking some beef ribs till they were good and tender. Then she added diced onions and potatoes, shredded cabbage, ripe tomatoes, carrots, celery, corn, chopped string beans, diced green and red peppers, lima beans, rice, barley, and parsley leaves. Like it or not, Mary was going to receive a home-cooked present from her shunned friend sometime soon.

While the soup simmered, she dusted the front room, then took out the rugs and beat them against the tree trunk in front of the house. She thought of combining her stop at Mary's, tomorrow or the next day, with a brief visit to Dat and Mamma, but decided against it. Thinking of the old home place—not having laid eyes on it in such a long time—she felt sad. Typically, at such times, she'd take herself out to visit friends, attend a work frolic, or, if nothing else, simply get out under the sky and look up at the trees. Experiencing the peace of the countryside and a long talk with the Lord, she would often feel better in a short time. Which is what she decided to do the minute the soup was well cooked; some of it put away for her own lunch and a large portion of it stowed away in the freezer, for Bishop John's Mary.

Upstairs, she adjusted her prayer veiling at the bureau mirror, noticing a note from Dan. Along with the note, several checks had been left for her to deposit at the bank. *Would you mind taking these for me . . . if you have time today? Love to you—Dan.*

Daniel. What a considerate, dear husband. Still courting her by his words and deeds, even though they'd been married nearly a full year. She wondered what she might bake special to surprise him on their first wedding anniversary in a few weeks. Not one for cake, Dan *did* love his pies. And what an assortment of recipes she had to choose from. Fruit pies, cream pies, and the ever-popular shoofly pie—Great-Aunt Ella Mae's recipe.

Eager to help with the bank errand, Katie headed up Cattail Road, driving toward Route 340, then turned in the direction of the village of Intercourse. She found herself glad for the chance to get out, in spite of the bleak, cool day, unusual for mid-autumn in Lancaster County. Sunshine and blue skies typically reigned for weeks on end, a luster of fall colors abounding on every hand. Not today.

As she drove she contemplated her life with Dan. What a truly amazing thing—their love story. Had she any interest in writing at all, she might've put pen to paper, describing how they'd lost each other for five long years, then found each other only to be kept apart by one unforeseen circumstance after another. God, in His great sovereignty and wisdom, had planned for them to be united as husband and wife. She strongly believed this.

Tonight I'll talk to Dan . . . share my struggle, she thought as she parked the car and got out, hurrying to the bank.

Opening the door to the main entrance, she saw that the place was nearly empty of people. She walked up to one of the two tellers and deposited the checks into her and Dan's joint account.

That done, she headed out the main doors, fully concentrating on the parking lot and the short walk to her car. It was then she noticed a young man of medium build and slicked-back blond hair, who closely resembled her unmarried brother. A second look, and she was *sure* it was Benjamin—with an English girl at his side. Another furtive glance and her gaze registered the tie-dyed T-shirt, blue jeans, and high-topped tennis shoes.

She was tempted to call out "Hullo, Ben" but thought better of it. Waiting until the couple went into the bank and were out of sight, Katie walked over to a red sports car—prob'ly belonging to the girl—and peered through the windows. The console was decked out with an array of things: radio, tape player, and what might be one of those newfangled CD players. She gave the car's interior a once-over, her breath catching in her throat when she spied a pack of cigarettes lying in a compartment next to some loose change.

Well, if this doesn't beat all, she thought, hoping against hope her brother hadn't taken up the smoking habit.

Not wanting to cause a scene, she quickly retreated to her own car and sat behind the wheel, waiting for Ben and his girlfriend to come out of the bank. Lingering there, she recalled her encounter on the road with Dat and Benjamin, the morning of Eli's wedding. Ben, she recalled, seemed downright put out with her. He'd rushed to the horse, trying to control the animal. Yet it was the peculiar way he had glanced out of the corner of his eye at her while Dat struggled with the reins . . . Ben's angry words, *"What're you doin' here, Katie?"*

Ben, after all, had been the brother closest in age to her, the sibling who'd playfully teased her, both at work and play. On their long walk to school, at both morning and afternoon milking, on the way to church—no matter—Ben was always the one bantering or poking fun at her.

When her brother and the English girl emerged from the bank, walking hand-in-hand across the parking lot, she had only to watch Ben's mannerisms—hear his raucous laughter— to know he was acting like a teenager in the middle of *Rumschpringa*—the running-around years. Truth be known, Ben was close to twenty-six, much too old for such immature behavior. Goodness' sakes, he was well into marrying age, though she'd heard that Ben's sweetheart had jilted him for another. One of the hollow's own girls. Well, no wonder he was strutting round with a fancy Englischer!

What on earth was he doing? Didn't he know such con- duct would ultimately break Mam's and Dat's hearts? Hadn't they suffered enough already, Katie herself having left the Amish church behind and all? Katie wanted to leap out of the car, tell him just how sorry she was, that she prayed for him daily.

Yet something restrained her, and she knew in her soul that Ben's situation was far different from her own. She *had* sown some wild oats as a teenager, playing her forbidden guitar and longing for fancy clothes and things. But she'd never puffed on cigarettes or run with worldly boys. In the end, *her* reason for abandoning the Amish lifestyle had more to do with spiritual precepts and beliefs than a rebellious attitude. 'Least it was from her way of thinking.

Bewildered at what a day can bring forth, she drifted into deep thought, unaware that her brother must've spotted her and was now approaching her car. He knocked on the window on the driver's side, peering down at her.

"Oh!" she shrieked.

He motioned for her to lower the window. Quickly, she turned on the ignition to access the power, scarcely knowing what to say.

"Listen here, Katie. You haven't seen me today, do you understand?" he said.

"Benjamin . . . I—"

"Don't tell anyone 'bout my car, ya hear?"

She frowned, confused.

"Promise me this!" he demanded.

"What's going on, Ben?" she asked softly.

"None of your business." He flattened the sides of his hair with both palms, reeking of a blend of aftershave and cigarette smoke. "Now, will ya promise you won't say anything to Mam? I know she calls ya ev'ry so often."

She wondered how he knew. "Our parents aren't fools, in case you think you can pull the wool over their eyes."

"I ain't callin' anyone a fool." His voice was tense. "Just keep quiet 'bout this."

"Well, if this is the life you're choosing, I suggest you keep your car very well hidden. 'Cause sooner or later you'll get caught."

"How can ya know that?"

She watched him closely. A nervous twitch in his cheek revealed his uncertainty. He *hadn't* made the choice to go fancy. Not yet anyway. "What about your baptismal vow, your promise to God and the church?"

"You should talk!" He leaned both hands on her window, looking down and shaking his head.

"Ben . . . listen. The Amish life is all you know."

"There's much more to this," he barked.

She eyed him, praying silently for wisdom. "I think we should spend some time together . . . it's been ever so long." This was risky for him, she knew, but so was traipsing round with Jezebel. "Come over and have lunch with me," she pleaded.

"At *your* place?"

She gave him quick directions. "Drop by tomorrow . . . anytime, really."

He didn't say he would or wouldn't, just turned on his heels and left.

On the drive home from the bank, the sky was a drab gray-white, not a speck of color. The air was still, not a trace of wind. The overall mood of the day reflected her inner struggle. 'Course, Katie had no right to admonish her brother, older than herself by nearly two years. Yet, she *did* have something to offer, far more priceless than mere good advice.

The road sloped gently down toward Hickory Hollow, toward the wooded area where she and her brothers Eli and Benjamin, and sometimes their eldest brother, Elam, had often played hidey-go-seek in summer, chased after chipmunks in autumn, and followed each other's footprints in the snow during wintertime. Where the pond met both the woods and the wagon roads, out behind the two-story bank barn, there was a special place—"a world set apart." It was the only spot to row a boat, "to drift away the cares of the day," Mary Stoltzfus sometimes liked to say, a watering hole where all three brothers—sometimes Dat, too—picked up their long willow sticks and went fishing of a morning.

The whole of the village, it seemed, was beset with memories. Too many to count. She passed up making the turn toward the hollow, instead heading away from the Plain village, driving toward the cozy house she and Daniel called home. Another day she'd drop in on Mary with the frozen vegetable soup. Not this day. This gray and miserable day.

Thinking again of Benjamin and the possibility of his visit, she prayed, *Lord, may it be so. Tomorrow . . .*

At supper Katie mentioned to Dan having run into Benjamin at the bank. "Sad to say, but he's flirting with the world." She described Ben's ultracontemporary getup and hairstyle, his heavily made-up girlfriend, his own brash attitude.

Dan listened, not as quick to judge. "Sounds like the Lord

is at work, you running into him like that." He paused, smiling. "Don't forget, we've been praying for our families. This may be the beginning of something."

Hearing her husband talk this way gave her even more hope. "If Ben drops by tomorrow, I'll share the love of the Lord Jesus with him. For sure and for certain."

Dan was in agreement and promised to be in prayer for her. They continued to eat, but Katie felt tense. She wanted to bring up her and Mam's phone conversation just now, but she let a few more moments pass.

Then, breathing deeply, she forged ahead. "Mam tells me that Dat wouldn't mind if I came by the house for a short visit sometime." She chose her words carefully so as not to hurt him, though she doubted he could be further pained by Samuel Lapp excluding him from a casual visit. Not with Dan's own parents having severely rejected him and still standing their ground. "I thought it best we talk it over," she said.

Dan's eyes were suddenly bright. "If the door's truly open, why not go?"

Well, the door sure seemed to be open. "Can we pray about it?" she asked.

He reached for her hand and held it in both of his. "You seem a bit hesitant." His eyes searched hers. "Are you all right, Katie?"

"I just want to do the right thing." Truth be known, she welcomed the chance to visit. More than anything, she wanted to be a witness of God's saving grace to both her parents. All the family, really.

"I don't view the invitation as a negative thing. Not at all." Dan was attentive, his face more serious now as they ate their dessert at the small square table next to the kitchen window. "You decide. It's completely up to you."

He didn't seem a bit put off, and she was relieved. "I only wish Mam had included *you* . . . that they respected our marriage that much," she said.

He smiled tenderly, stroking her hand. "If you choose to go, make whatever connection you can for the glory of God. Don't worry about me."

She fought back tears. "Could be the first step to uniting our families."

"The matter is in God's hands," Dan said with confidence.

Where it belongs, she thought.

When noontime came the next day, and no sign of Benjamin, she set the table for herself, ate a bowl of vegetable soup and a toasted cheese sandwich, then, drawing hot water into the sink, she washed the single bowl, the utensils, and her water glass. Thinking that today, being the sky blue sunny day it was, she might venture over to Hickory Hollow, at least stop in and deliver the frozen soup to Mary. Maybe wait another day to visit Mam and Dat—she just didn't know.

Having packed up the frozen chunk of soup, she placed the cardboard box on the kitchen table and hurried out to the utility room, where she took down a woolen sweater from a wooden peg and slipped her arms into its sleeves.

She drove past the woodland area near her parents' farmhouse, not permitting herself to dwell on the former days of childhood play. Not even turning once to glance at the red sandstone farmhouse coming up on the right. Today she would keep her thoughts in check. She had a purpose, a mission to accomplish. She was here, in the hollow, on an errand of mercy. When she dropped off the homemade soup, she would offer only a cheerful smile. "How're you doing, Mary? 'S'nice to see you again." That sort of thing. Having not seen her friend for a full year now, the last thing Katie wanted to do was burden dear Mary.

Once she had all that worked out in her mind, things didn't seem so bleak as yesterday. 'Course, *this* day being what it was, all sunny and warm—skies blue as the blue of the ocean at the horizon line—her spirits were lifted.

Katie knocked on the back door, and when Mary came she stood in the window momentarily before opening the door. "Katie . . . it's you," she said, eyes filled with a mixture of sad-ness and joy.

"So good to see you, Mary." She held the cardboard box, staring down at it. "I made more vegetable soup than we can hope to eat . . . thought you and your family might enjoy some."

Mary's mouth dropped open. She eyed Katie's parcel and stepped aside. "Come in, won'tcha?" Mary beckoned.

Due to shunning practices, Katie knew better than to hand the soup directly to Mary, from her hands to a member in good standing in the Amish church. Just wasn't done. She went no farther than the utility room and set the box down on a shelf in the small outer room.

"Denki—thank you," Mary said of the soup.

"Hope you enjoy it."

"I'm sure we will." Mary didn't seem to know what to do with her hands. First, she folded them, then put them behind her back, swaying like a shy schoolgirl.

The house seemed awfully quiet. Was the bishop home or not? Katie wondered.

Mary must've sensed her concern. Quickly, she explained that John was out delivering shoes for horses to several farmers at the north end of the hollow.

"How's everybody?" Katie asked.

"Oh, we're fine," Mary said. "Can ya stay?"

"Only a minute." Katie struggled with the reality of the situation.

"How are you and Dan?" asked Mary.

"We're fine . . . thanks for asking."

Katie went on to inquire about the children, and Mary's response was short and to the point. The children were in good health, it seemed, and the chores were attended to daily, as well as plenty of book learnin' going on under the bishop's roof. But looking at her dear friend, Katie was a bit worried. The light was gone from Mary's eyes, the cheery-cheeked complexion sadly absent. "How are you, *really?*" Katie pressed.

Mary was silent for a moment. Then, slowly . . . ever so slowly, it happened. The former bond of friendship took over, and they began to talk softly, best friends kept apart by a society's rules and regulations. "I have good days and bad . . . like everyone else, I 'spect," Mary admitted.

"Well, you aren't sick, I hope."

Mary's lip quivered. "Just a bit wore out, that's all."

"I didn't come to cause you pain. You must know that."

"No . . . no . . . it was right thoughtful of you to come, Katie."

"I wish there was more I could do. You surely have your hands full . . . my dear friend."

Mary smiled through her tears. "Your mam offered to help. And the older children—Hickory John and Nancy—are gut 'bout helping when they're home."

They talked a blue streak. But they were cautious, even wise, steering clear of the differences in their beliefs . . . doctrines, too. Meanwhile, the vegetable soup was starting to thaw. "I s'pose we could chew the fat all day, jah?" Mary said, hurrying to put away the soup.

From where she stood, Katie could see into the kitchen, the long table stretching out under the windows on one side, a gas lamp hanging overhead, and the wood stove opposite the table and benches. Same layout as Mamma's. "I best be going," she said.

"Wish you could stay . . . wish *we* could . . ." Mary's voice trailed off, and she leaned hard against the wall.

"You sure you're all right?" Katie asked before leaving. "You just look so tired."

"Oh, I'm fine," Mary said, though Katie wasn't convinced. There were dark circles under Mary's eyes, prob'ly from lack of sleep or from pushing herself much too hard. Maybe both.

Mary thanked her repeatedly for such a "wonderful-gut deed."

Just as Katie was turning to go, Mary said that one of the

elders had spotted a red car parked out behind the Miller's house, "over on the west side of the hollow."

She listened, a bit surprised that Mary would bring up such a topic, especially considering Katie's status among the People. But she volunteered nothing.

"The car's parked over at Peter and Lydia Miller's place of a night."

The homestead belonged to her mother's second cousins— churchgoing Mennonites. "Ben's in need of prayer," Katie said, fumbling for the right words.

"I'm afraid he's got one foot in the world and one in the church . . . ownin' a car and all. Next thing the car will own *him*."

Katie sighed. This was terribly awkward. "Ben's searching, that's what I think."

"But . . . all your brother needs is right here with the People," Mary spoke her mind.

Amish ways had been well ingrained in Katie, yet her heart had longed for more than man-made rules and traditions could offer. She'd best be careful what she said now.

"Surely you haven't gone and influenced Ben . . . away from the church, I mean."

Katie let it be known she'd had nothing to do with Ben's disobedience. And with that, she opened the door to go.

"Ach . . . I'm awful sorry, Katie. Truly, I am." Mary reached out her hand. "Didn't mean to cast blame on ya."

Katie gripped her friend's hand.

"You are so kind to come." Mary sniffled.

She wished she could open her heart and reveal to Mary that she *did* hope to influence Benjamin someday, for the Lord.

Mary too. In fact, Katie prayed daily that she might lead each and every one of the People to Jesus, just as the Wise Woman had led her.

◆

As tempted as Katie was to stare at the long lane leading to Dat and Mam's house, she kept going, past the old stone house where she'd grown up. Where Samuel and Rebecca Lapp had brought her home as a newborn infant to be their adopted daughter. She even nixed the urge to glimpse the Millers' barnyard, where Ben's shiny sports car was said to be hiding.

She drove without stopping, all the way out to the intersection that ultimately led her to the clapboard house. Past the wide meadows and the creek running through it, where she made her home with Dan. As she drove, she prayed for Mary. "Provide for her every need, dear Lord, spirit, mind, and body." Oh, how she longed to have a spiritual connection with her lifelong friend. Sharing the Lord brought people together in a way like no other. Surely God, in His sovereign plan, wouldn't allow them to grow up together only to drift apart as young adults. And right around the time when one, or both of them, might become expectant mothers. In fact, she had a feeling Mary was already expecting her first baby—hers and John's. Was that the reason for her friend's fatigue?

Thinking back on the visit, she recalled that Mary had offered her nothing to eat or drink. Not even a glass of water. Just as well. The bishop's wife was abiding by the rules of the shunning. Katie couldn't find fault in that.

◆

The car parked in the driveway took Katie off guard, but only for a moment as she pulled in, then turned off the ignition. Getting out, she noticed Benjamin perched on the gazebo steps in the side yard.

"Have you been here long?" she asked, walking toward him.

"A quarter hour or so."

She had hoped he might come earlier, for lunch, but seeing him now was enough to make her smile. "Come in, come in," she said, hurrying around to the back door.

They sat together in the kitchen, occasionally looking out over the pastureland from the window, two cups of coffee and a plate of sticky buns between them. "Don't know why I'm here, really," he confessed between bites.

She nodded at him, this brother of hers, who looked so peculiar in his polished cowboy boots and tight blue jeans. Actually, the clothing she could almost overlook, but the gunked-up hair struck her as downright comical. She didn't laugh. Laughter would be a dire mistake.

Silently, she listened as he began to share the pressures he was feeling at home. "Comes mostly from Dat," he said. "'Cept Mam brought it up the other day...'bout me taking over the farm, livin' on their side of the house, me and the girl I marry. But I don't have my eye on any Plain girls just now."

Katie could think of a handful of Amish girls she'd suspected him of courting on and off through the years—before the girl who'd hurt him so awful bad. But she felt it best to keep her peace. Let Ben voice his feelings, speak out his frustrations.

Looking at him sitting across the table from her, his eyes intent on life, his hair all shiny and hard from whatever it was he was smearing on it these days—well, she had a strong notion he needed to get some things off his chest.

"Dat's itchin' to slow down some." Ben stared at his coffee. "But why do I hafta plan *my* life round the old man's decision to retire?"

Katie wasn't too surprised. She'd heard him fussing in the past enough to know he sometimes got riled up.

"What if Eli took over instead?" she suggested. "Anyone thought of that?"

Ben shook his head. "Eli's got himself a carpentry shop out in the shed behind their new place. I daresay he'll make a gut livin' doing what he enjoys. Besides, Eli's never been too keen on farming."

She wondered if the strain coming from Dat was the reason Ben wanted to experience the world—buying himself a car and going with the English girl. "What if Dat wasn't planning to retire for a while?" she said, thinking that Ben needed time to find himself, maybe.

"Wouldn't make me any difference." He took his time drinking his coffee. Then—"I'm thinking of leaving the church, Katie."

"For what reason?" she asked, a bit shocked.

"Tell ya the truth, I'm fed up." He drew a deep breath. "Need to get out on my own."

She was cautious. Ben was clearly upset at the world, not just at their father. "Is this about your girlfriend leaving you for—"

"*You* got shunned, Katie, and you're doin' all right!"

She shook her head. "You're wrong about that." She breathed a prayer for wisdom. "Let me tell you something. There isn't a day that goes by that I'm not cut off from my family, from all the People . . . my dearest friend, Mary, too. I live with the pain each and every day. Yet there is nothing I can do to change it. I'm a follower of the Lord Jesus, and there's no turning back for me."

"Same as you, I have no choice but to leave."

"Well, if you were leaving the Old Order to follow the Lord—to accept His gift of salvation—I'd encourage you. But I'm not sure that's what you mean to do."

Ben was silent, head down.

Katie was caught in the snare of a dilemma. Here was Ben ripe for the picking, perhaps hungry for the fullness of the Lord. Yet he wasn't talking about leaving the tradition of the People for the sake of the Gospel. "I do pray that someday you'll find the peace I've found in Jesus, Ben. You're a young man in rebellion to your father," she said. "If you feel you must leave the Plain life behind, be sure to count the cost. *Be sure you know why you're willing to go fancy.*"

By the time Dan arrived home from work, Katie had bid Ben, "*Gut-n-Owed*—Good evening." Reluctant to see her brother go, she called after him, "The door's always open here for you." But he hurried down the steps toward his car without promising to return.

Dan was quite interested in her account of Ben's visit. "I was in prayer off and on all day," he told her.

"And I surely felt your prayers," she said as she set the table. "Ben's clearly searching for truth. I just hope he doesn't do something he'll be sorry for later."

They talked a bit more about Ben's visit, then Dan swept her into his arms. "How was the rest of your day?"

"I stopped in to see Mary. Took her a batch of vegetable soup."

He smiled. "I'm sure she was surprised to see you."

She told how they'd talked and wept. Heartbreaking, it was. Yet in another way the short visit had been ever so sweet. "Mary 'n' Katie," she whispered. "Not two peas in a pod the way it used to be . . . but our special bond's still there all the same."

Two days later Katie was both surprised and delighted to see Ben's car pull up in the driveway around eleven-thirty. "Well, come in, stranger . . . you're just in time for lunch."

He appeared to be more at ease this visit, and she had him sit at the head of the table. She served him baked macaroni and cheese and a veal loaf. "Looks like I'm breakin' bread with a shunned church member," he said.

"We can set up separate tables if you'd rather," she suggested, wondering if he was already under a probationary Bann, due to his comment.

"No need for that." Ben bowed his head, leading in the silent prayer.

After the "amen," it dawned on her that today Ben's hair was free of the goo, washed out clean.

"What're ya starin' at?" he asked.

"Your hair's all clean and shiny." She passed the platter of veal to him. "I daresay you're looking more like an Amishman again."

He said not a word.

"I'm thinking I might go over to visit Mam and Dat this afternoon," she said, changing the subject.

"Do they know you're comin'?"

"Suppose not, but they shouldn't be *too* surprised."

"Why's that?" he asked.

She shared with him the invitation Mam had offered. "Just why is it, do you think, they don't mind me coming now . . . their shunned daughter, and all?"

"For one thing, Dat's not as *absenaat*—headstrong—as he's been in the past. Doesn't show his indignation so much anymore, neither."

She thought on that. "I wonder why."

"It's you, Katie . . . he's lost his only girl to the church's rulebook. Why else?"

"What would Bishop John say if he knew?" she asked.

"Dat won't be tellin' the bishop, I guarantee ya that." His eyes were blinking to beat the band. "Dat's been sitting for the longest time of an evening, reading the Bible, a-turnin' one page after another."

So then her shunning had its virtues, after all. Her heart leaped for joy over Ben's remark.

"Don't be quotin' me on that," he said.

She had to smile. Her brother was telling stories out of school, and Dat wouldn't be any too pleased. "My lips are sealed."

After dessert Katie brought up the thorny subject. "The bishop knows about your car."

"Who said so?"

"A little bird."

He hung his head. "Didn't think the People would find out so awful quick."

"It's not too late to confess . . . to change the direction of your life." She reached across to touch his arm.

He sighed audibly. "Don't rightly know what to do."

"Have you ever searched the Scriptures for divine guidance?"

He shook his head. "Prob'ly, I'll end up shunned," Ben muttered.

"All for good reason, if you choose God's way."

He scooted back from the table. "And if I keep my car and my fancy girlfriend I'll get kicked out, too. Either way, I'm banned."

She could see he was downright miserable.

He said he felt justified in owning a car and driving it, " 'specially when one of Preacher's sons has unnecessary reflectors and decorations all over his buggy. One sin's as bad as another, ain't?"

She thought on that. "Maybe owning a car isn't as wrong as wanting it so," she said.

"Truth be told, I don't know what I want anymore." He was awful quiet for the longest time.

"The Lord loves you, Ben. Why don't you ask Him to lead you?"

He looked her straight in the eye. "I . . . uh, would you do it *for* me?"

"Right now, you mean?"

He agreed, nodding his head.

She prayed a gentle, compassionate prayer, requesting God's help in the life of her precious brother. When she finished, tears glistened in Ben's eyes. "I'm awful proud of you," she said.

" 'Pride goeth before a fall,' " he said flatly, a hint of a smile on his face.

"Oh, go on. You know what I mean."

His face turned ever so serious then. "Jah, I believe so, Katie," he said. "I believe I do."

◆

Ben's visit gave her the boost she needed to drive over to see her parents. Mam's and Dat's faces were unsmiling as she shared about her doings at church and Daniel's work as a draftsman.

After a time Mam said, "Benjamin was just here and left with the horse and carriage."

Dat nodded. "He finally wants to talk farming. On our land."

"That's good," she said cautiously.

Dat continued. "The land is God's greatest gift to mankind. Never does it betray you. The longer you live on the land, the more you'll come to love it."

Katie wondered what Dat was getting at. Was this his way of speaking his mind in so many words? This was surely a different way than she'd ever known Dat to be.

Mam's eyes sparkled. A curious frown crossed her brow. "You wouldn't happen to know 'bout Ben's sudden interest in farming, would ya?"

She wouldn't let on. She'd given Benjamin her word. "Some young men take longer to mature than others, that's all," Katie said.

"Well, now, ain't *that* the truth!" Dat was in total agreement.

"Is that true of young women, too?" Mam asked.

Katie was prepared for this, for Mam to bring up the topic one way or another. Every time they talked by phone, lately, Mam was saying something to this effect. So why would she overlook the opportunity in her own house? 'Specially with Dat here to back her up?

"I don't mean that you're not mature," Mam added. "Just would be awful nice if *you* returned to the People, Katie. You and Daniel both . . . reestablished in the church community."

"I don't have to attend the Amish church to belong to the Lord." She put it as gently as she knew how. "Dan and I gladly offer our lives and our talents to God's work. For His glory."

Her father was fidgety, as if he wanted to debate the issue in the worst way. But he kept a-rockin' in his chair, shaking his head every now and then. Not once did he agree with her, not at all, yet something about his eyes made her wonder if he

97

was softening to her just a bit. Maybe so . . .

When the time came to leave, she hugged Mam, but Dat hung back, cautious of getting too close to his wayward girl, no doubt.

"You'll hafta drop by sometime again," Mam said softly.

Just not too soon. . . . Katie thought.

She headed to the back door. "The same road goes to Dan's and my house, same as here, you know," she said quickly.

Neither parent commented on her parting words. Just as well. Best to let them mull things over a bit, come to a conclusion in their own way. And in their time.

A westerly breeze stirred the trees as she made her way to the car. Overhead, transparent clouds skimmed the sky. In a few hours, twilight would fall over Hickory Hollow and beyond.

As she drove she wondered about running into Benjamin at the bank. Surely the encounter had been divine providence at work. Was it also the makings of the long road back to her father's heart? She'd keep trusting the Lord for that.

But she wouldn't be sharing with her parents anytime soon how she'd talked sense to their youngest son. Or that she believed wholeheartedly that prayer had brought Benjamin across her path. Even to her very door. No need.

The glory was God's and His alone.

By Lantern's Light

Joy is the sweet voice, joy the luminous cloud—
We in ourselves rejoice!
All thence flows all that charms or ear or sight,
All melodies the echoes of that voice,
All colors a suffusion from that light.

—Samuel Taylor Coleridge

The idea had come to her in the early evening, just as the last vestiges of sunbeams winked over the horizon and disappeared out of sight. Mary savored the thought, keeping it hidden safely inside, wishing not to share it with another soul.

In three days her dearest friend—Katie Lapp Fisher—would celebrate her first wedding anniversary. 'Course, the celebration would be a far cry from what it might've been had Katie and Dan repented and returned to the community of the People. Yet Mary hadn't washed her hands of the dear couple, no. She'd grown up in the hollow with both Katie *and* Daniel, shared many a happy day during their years spent at the one-room school, enjoyed a good many fall afternoons in her early teens, raking and gatherin' up leaves, then havin' a big bonfire over at the Lapp farmhouse, all the while aware of Daniel's fond and frequent smiles directed toward Katie.

Had Katie confessed and married Daniel Fisher under the covering of the Amish church, why, they'd be invited to a big anniversary dinner of scalloped ham or Swiss steak over at Samuel and Rebecca Lapp's place, no doubt, come this Saturday noon. And, too, invitations would have been extended all round to Dan's immediate family and to Katie's brothers and families, as well as to Mary herself and her husband, John.

She emerged from the back door and hurried out across the back lawn strewn with fallen oak leaves, murky and rust-red in the growing dusk. One year of wedded happiness for Katie and Dan. Think of it! Katie would be expecting her first baby here perty soon. Maybe she already was, though nothing had been said when she dropped by unexpectedly with homemade soup a while back.

Mary headed to the barn in search of her husband's full-size farm lantern. She needed some time to herself, time to let her thoughts wander a bit. Just a short walk down one of the mule roads. Not too far. While her dried beef casserole was baking in the wood stove, she would go. While her husband and the boys, Hickory John and Levi, rode home from mending a pasture fence for one of John's cousins; while the girls, Nancy and Susie, redd up the kitchen and set the table, shooing Jacob, a big tease, from the kitchen till the evening meal was served.

She wondered what it might be like to celebrate the first-year milestone as someone who'd known the Old Ways but "turned fancy"—choosing modern life over a solid Amish upbringing, and of their own free will yet. Honestly, she *couldn't* imagine doing such a thing herself, but she tried to envision Katie preparing a big meal for Daniel, lighting candles on the table—just for looks. More than likely, they enjoyed all the comforts of modern conveniences. Electric lights and fancy kitchen appliances, telephones, even radios—bein' Mennonites now, and all. Mary was fairly certain of this, yet she'd never been inside their home. Though once she'd driven horse and buggy, secretly, past the house.

Plodding through the barnyard, she held John's heavy lantern in hand, following the wide circle of light beneath her feet and beyond. City folk—even English farmers—hadn't any idea just how dark the hollow got at night. They had their streetlights, lamps burning in houses and stores. No need for gas lamps or lanterns. Took electricity for granted, prob'ly, so handy it was.

Sometimes she and John sat out on the front porch, staring at the farmland, acres and acres of darkness, 'specially on a night with no moon. An evening such as this. 'Course, she couldn't see past the long miles it would take to look into the bustling city of Lancaster. But she knew there were radiant lights ablaze on every street corner and some in between, too. She knew this because she had ridden into town on occasion. Not in a buggy through the busy narrow streets—not only unsafe, but unwise. She had gone in a van driven by a Mennonite man, heading to Central Market downtown. Several times she had traveled the highway to visit some of Mamma's distant cousins in Newburg, south of Harrisburg.

Lookin' up at the stars, sometimes Mary and her husband would see a giant beacon cast its rays of light against the black sky, slowly moving round and round, the power of its brilliance beyond her understanding. "It's some English folk having a carnival somewhere . . . or maybe a car lot sale," John would say, his only explanation for the wasteful display.

So English city folk worked and lived and spent their hours under bright lights, a world she did not comprehend, nor care to. Mary wondered if any of their elderly family members remembered back to gas lanterns or candles on the table. Did any of them miss the quietude an ink black night could afford? Did they recall how difficult it was writing a letter or reading a recipe book by candlelight?

All day long the land seemed to glow with the light of the sun shinin' down. During the day a body never thought twice 'bout how dark the world would be come nightfall. The minute the sun set, the People went out to get their gas lamps, carrying them into the kitchen to brighten things up a bit. Life truly revolved around the light.

Her thoughts turned back to Katie and Dan. On the morning of their first anniversary, would Daniel go looking for Katie in the kitchen, say to her with a big smile, "Happy day, dear!"? Would he then sit at the table while Katie served him a big breakfast of fresh cantaloupe, and strawberries, too, griddle cakes, eggs on toast, and black coffee? Halfway through the meal, Dan might get up from the table and lean down and give his sweetheart girl a kiss. And Katie, pleased as punch, might be thinkin' all the while of the gift he surely had waiting for her, along with the special one she'd purchased for him, havin' saved up money for several months from takin' in sewing, along with her baked-goods money, no doubt. Then while Katie washed and dried dishes, she might think of the anniversary greetings sure to arrive in the day's mail. A good many would come from the hollow, from Katie's immediate family, as well as dozens of extended family members. There would be a card from Mary, too, wishing Katie "many happy years ahead," the handwritten note might say, though Mary truly wished she might write something more along the lines of "Looking forward to seeing you soon," or "Wish we could help you celebrate."

Setting the lantern down, she left it there on the ground and headed out into the dark field. She craned her neck, looking at the sky, at wee twinkles of light in the far-flung heavens, too dim to make a difference on the mule path she trod.

When she'd gone more than an acre away from the golden sphere of light, she turned and stared back at John's lantern. "Oh, Katie, how can you be so awful stubborn?" she whispered into the stillness. "Why'd you hafta go and botch things up so?"

She sighed. Alone in the grazing land, Mary kept her face toward the distant lantern light, recalling her own first anniversary celebration some months back. John had surprised her with a handmade hickory rocker. Such a wonderful-gut present it was. He had acted almost *schofisch*—sheepish—about the gift, standing back as she tried it out, rocking back and forth, just grinnin' up at him. "Do ya like it?" he'd said, keeping his eyes on her. "Suits me just fine, and . . . it's right perty, too," she'd said happily, waiting for him to come and pull her up out of the rocking chair and gather her into his arms. He had kissed her with more passion than she'd become accustomed to lately, and with that she had to sit back down in the rocker, catching her breath just a bit, as he smiled at her.

She wondered how they might celebrate their fiftieth wedding anniversary. Fifty years of devotion to each other—lovin' each other, their blended family, and by then, dozens of grandchildren, Lord willing—that, along with having served and ministered to the People here in the hollow for half a century. *If* the Good Lord saw fit to give them that many years. She didn't ever want to take such a thing for granted. Never.

Standing there in the middle of the meadow, she wondered what John would think of her idea to bake a pie and take it over to Katie. She didn't hafta guess too hard to know. Then again, she wouldn't go behind John's back, though she was awful sure her bishop husband would oppose her payin' Katie a visit.

But, oh, she longed to see where her friend lived, shunning or no. She'd give most anything to do so. If not this week, someday.

As for *this* day, she had ever such gut news for John, the minute the house was quiet. After supper, prob'ly, when everyone was tucked into bed. Their firstborn child—theirs together—was to be born next spring. Scarcely could she think on it without joyful tears.

The night was growing chilly now, and she clung to her shawl, pulling it up round her shoulders. Best be getting back to the house, put finishing touches on the meal. She picked up her pace, making her way toward the lantern's glow. Her eye caught shimmers of light out on the road as they bobbed along equal to the speed of a horse and carriage, winging its way toward hearth and home.

John! Her heart leaped up at the thought of both the present and the future . . . the tiny babe growing within her. She cherished the strange yet precious life-flutters, a fusion of hope and love. John's new son or daughter tucked just beneath her own heart.

The dark outline of the house became more evident as she approached the lantern and stooped to pick it up. Pausing, she took simple pleasure in the dim barnyard ahead, aware of the single gas lamp reflected in the kitchen windows. Not a powerful beacon, still it shone, poking holes in the face of night.

Her splendid idea of going to see Katie in her modern house seemed somehow less urgent now. Why, she'd simply bake a special anniversary pie and take it over to Rebecca Lapp. It would give Katie's mamma a gut excuse to ride horse and buggy over there.

Jah, 'tis a better idea, she thought, going to the barn and returning John's lantern. Then Mary hurried across the yard, up the back steps, and into the house.

A Gift to Remember

The holiest of all holidays are those
Kept by ourselves in silence and apart;
The secret anniversaries of the heart.

—*Henry Wadsworth Longfellow*

Katie heard the phone ringing from where she stood under the rose arbor cutting down the last of the dried vines. Clippers in hand, she hurried up the gentle slope of the back lawn and into the house. Picking up the phone, she answered, "Hullo?"

"This is Bash Jewelers calling. May I speak to Katie Fisher?"

"This is Katie."

"Your special order is in," the jeweler said. "You may pick it up at your convenience."

"Thank you." She hung up the phone, thinking what a wonderful-gut surprise the new watch would be for Dan on the occasion of their first wedding anniversary. In just two days.

There were a good many things she must do between now and then. Setting the clippers down on the kitchen counter, she took from her sweater pocket a folded piece of paper marked *Anniversary List* at the top. She'd made a rather long list for the occasion to keep herself on track, jotting down everything she could possibly think of, hopin' the day might go off without a hitch. In addition to having the house tip-top clean, she also planned to cook a nice hot meal to be served at five o'clock in the evening, complete with candles and her best china and silverware, all done up in the dining room. Just for the two of them. 'Course, if circumstances had been different—were she and Dan not under the Bann—they would, most likely, be celebrating their anniversary around Mamma's big trestle table in her enormous kitchen, eating with loved ones and friends. As it was, she *had* thought of inviting their minister, who'd married them at the old Mennonite meeting-house, and his wife. Had even given thought to inviting the Freys, their new church friends. But, upon further reflection, she'd decided against it. No, this first year the celebrating would belong to them alone, a truly private event.

Ever since her recent visit with Darlene Frey, Katie had been eager to get things written down in an orderly fashion. The two women had spent a relaxing afternoon chatting on Darlene's porch swing, and Katie had made note of the quaint little swing for two, thinking what fun it would be to own one. That day Darlene had emphasized to her the need to prioritize a list, beginning with the most important items and working down. "That's the only way I'm able to juggle everything," she'd said.

So Katie had gone home and promptly written on the line beside the numeral one: *Gift for Dan.*

Weeks before she'd made a trip to the long-established

jewelers on North Queen Street in downtown Lancaster. After describing to the clerk what she was hoping to purchase, they found a fine watch with not one speck of gold edging on the face, ideal for a conservative Mennonite man. The wrist strap was a padded dark brown leather in a wide grain. "I'll take that one," she'd said, glad to have saved up money from taking in some sewing, as well as the sale of her baked goods, which she took to the small general store to be sold on consignment.

But, sadly, she discovered the watch was the last of its kind and must remain in the showcase. The clerk assured her they could order one exactly like it. "In time for my anniversary?" Katie asked. "Certainly!" was the enthusiastic reply.

She had ordered the watch, and now it had come in, ready to be purchased and picked up. Her heart quickened at the thought of Dan opening the gift. He certainly needed a new watch. The strap on the old one was beginning to fray; the clock face was scratched, too, thanks to years of drafting blueprints and whatnot.

Katie set about checking off the first item, Dan's gift, knowing full well that the watch could easily be gotten first thing tomorrow. Then she checked off other items farther down the list. *Purchase a three-inch steak.* Jah, she'd found a nice cut at the market. She would prepare it Saturday afternoon, following their noon meal.

Next, *seasonings*. A careful look at her pantry—each shelf lined with freshly canned vegetables, fruit, and preserves—and she spied parsley and ground pepper needed for her scalloped potatoes recipe, as well as some coconut and nutmeg for the coconut squash dish. Her eyes caught sight of a row of tall glass jars of asparagus and she decided, then and there, to add creamed asparagus to her menu for Saturday night. She also planned to make Mary's lime salad, a recipe from their teen years, which called for marshmallows and cream cheese, two ingredients she had written on her list. She would make sure she squeezed in a quick trip to the grocery store sometime today for those items. Yes, and she mustn't forget to pick up a lemon for Dan's favorite pie, her specialty: lemon sponge pie.

Besides redding up the house and tidying up the rose arbor, she must think ahead to preparing an early supper tonight as she had each evening this week, due to special meetings at church. Along with the two-hour meetings, there was to be a get-together this afternoon over at Darlene Frey's house for the church women's annual Fall Bake Sale, which Katie just so happened to be heading up.

She thought of her friend Mary managing *her* days, tending to the duties of a bishop's wife, as well as looking after five school-age children. No wonder the dear girl had appeared on the verge of exhaustion when last Katie visited. No wonder . . .

The thought of being an instant stepmother to five youngsters was enough to overwhelm her, and Katie was ever so grateful that, Lord willing, *her* babies would arrive one at a time, giving her and Dan ample opportunity to adjust to a new phase of life: parenting. Whenever the Lord saw fit to bless them, she was ready. And when their children *did* come, by then she would have Darlene's art of list-making all figured out.

Returning to the garden, Katie tended to the task of clipping away the dead vines, finishing the job in a few minutes. She stepped back to have a look. The arbor was ready for winter, and next spring there would be many more roses, to be sure. The tall, multi-sided birdhouse rose high in the center of the yard, towering over what had been beds of pansies and phlox and petunias. She liked to plant the same color together, making for a bold profusion of color in a flower bed. Something Mamma had always done.

Her thoughts flying off in tangents, Katie hurried to the potting shed. The tiny shelter was still wrapped in morning-glory vines on one side. Those ramblin' vines needed some tending to, as well. *Another day,* she thought. The garden shed bordered their backyard, offering a pleasant and sunny spot to start clippings and store clay pots and things. Quickly, she hung up the clippers and put her gardening gloves away in the top drawer of an old weathered cupboard she and Dan had found at an estate sale a while back.

Latching the small wooden door, she headed through the yard and up to the back porch. Indoors, she noticed her list lying on the kitchen counter and was glad to retrieve it. As Darlene had cautioned her, list-making was essential "for such an important day." She chuckled, thinking that both Mamma and Mary would prob'ly laugh out loud if they knew of the list. Why, she'd even taken time to include such things as: *peel potatoes, polish silverware,* and *set table.* Farther down on the list, of course. Still, they were things she normally remembered without a crutch. Duties that, as she'd told Darlene, "are second nature to me," she, having tended to housekeeping, cooking, baking, ironing, and, jah, peeling potatoes since she was fourteen or younger in Mamma's big kitchen.

Nevertheless, she slipped the list into her pocket, lest Dan return home early and discover too early all the lovely things she had planned. She couldn't dream of letting her surprises be spoiled by absentmindedness such as that.

First things first. She headed off to Darlene's for the meeting concerning the bake sale tomorrow. There, each of the women had lists of their own, and though Katie was in charge of the planning, she found herself wishing the get-together could be shortened somewhat, not develop into a teatime of sorts. She had so much to do.

"Would you mind terribly if I slip away?" she whispered to Darlene in the kitchen as her friend sliced a variety of apples and pears, placing them alongside a wide tray of cheese and crackers.

Darlene's face wrinkled up. "Aw, Katie, do you hafta go now . . . this soon?"

"I really hate to rush off, but I believe we've covered everything, and I really must make a stop at the grocery store before going home." It was then that she reminded Darlene of her anniversary. "It's this Saturday, you know."

Darlene's face broke into a broad grin. "Oh, that's right." She paused. "Well, if you've got a list—"

"Right here," Katie said, pulling it out and waving it.

"Then I should say you'll be fine." Darlene encouraged her to be on her way. "I'll finish things up here. Don't worry none."

Katie was ever so grateful and quickly said her good-byes to the womenfolk, assuring them that she'd see them first thing in the morning.

"We'll be seeing you tonight at church, too, won't we?" asked one.

"By all means." Katie thanked Darlene for her kindness and went out the back door. She made note of the sun's posi-

a clean dress and pulled on her best cotton sweater, thinking the evening might turn cooler, as she'd seen a V-shaped string of birds flying south this very day while working in the rose arbor. Unseasonably warm days couldn't last much longer. Yet she didn't bemoan the fact that wintry days were soon upon them. The shifting of seasons was likened unto a person's life, she knew. Perhaps God, in His infinite wisdom, had planned the remarkable parallel to remind us to prepare and plan for the inevitable. She wondered how many more years her own parents' good health would hold out. Would they come to walk in the fullness of God's grace before the winter of their lives came and went? Katie prayed it would be so.

———◆———

Friday morning, Katie got up hours before dawn and mixed the batter for one more cake and slid it into the oven for the bake sale.

Wash goblets. She scanned the remaining items on her list, feeling quite confident that she had time to do several chores before leaving for the bake sale. Quickly, she rinsed the water glasses, thinking they might be a bit soiled, and they were. The set had been a wedding gift from Dan's former boss and his wife. Only seldom were the glasses ever used, and now, thinking on it, she hadn't meant to wash all twelve glasses, not for just the two of them. But she was this far along, so why not?

After drying them, she returned the glasses to their appointed spot in the corner cupboard. Locating the white candles she'd purchased yesterday, Katie placed them on the buffet, in plain sight, so she'd remember. Then she checked to see that her white linen tablecloth and matching napkins were nicely ironed. They were.

She set to work polishing the best silverware, doing the same with all twelve place settings, even though she needed to polish only two. Humming as she worked, Katie wondered all the while what wonderful-gut surprise Dan surely had for her. Her darling had thrown out plenty of different options over the past weeks, so she couldn't be certain just what he had in mind. "A rocking chair would be nice," he'd said. "I think so, too," she'd agreed. A bit taken aback, he'd looked at her, a twinkle in his eyes. "Are you telling me something, Katie?" he asked. "Ach, not yet . . . but I hope soon," she replied.

Dan had also asked what sort of candies she liked best, along with remarks here and there about certain items of furniture. In the end, they had concluded there were plenty of furnishings for their home—"For now," Katie said.

'Course, part of the fun was the anticipation, waiting to see what the day might bring forth. Mamma had often said, *"You're much too curious a girl."* But that was years back, when she *was* too prying for her own good. Now, all grown-up and a young wife, Katie tried to quash her growing excitement. Dan had said not one word about any of his plans. Was his silence proof of something special? She wondered but wouldn't let herself get too caught up in the speculating, instead going about her duties, then checking the items off her list, sometimes two or three at a time.

"You'll be fine . . ." Darlene Frey's encouraging words rang in Katie's mind as she dry-mopped the hardwood floor in the

dining room. As the sun rose she gave the bay windows a quick once-over, these windows where she and Dan would look out together at the evening sky and the fields beyond. Tomorrow evening!

Come noon the church bake sale was already a big success. More than half the baked goods were bought up and some of the womenfolk were even accepting prepaid orders for specialty items like homemade teething cookies, soft pretzels, half-moon pies, and candies such as hardtack candy and taffy.

Darlene and several others at the long pie table got to talking about their wedding anniversaries, prob'ly because Katie had mentioned that her first was tomorrow. "Well, I didn't expect too much that first year," Darlene said, "'cept maybe flowers and some little candies, but my husband surprised me but good."

"What'd he give you?" one of the women asked.

"A brand-new bed," came the reply, which was met with laughter all round.

"If you'd ever spent a night in the old lumpy one, you'd know why a new bed was definitely in order," Darlene said, laughing.

Thinking on it, Katie was perty sure Dan wouldn't be buying a new bed. The one they had was perfectly fine.

Another woman howled with laughter as she chattered about *her* first wedding anniversary. "My husband jotted down the date on the calendar, but he put it on the wrong month, by mistake . . . so the day came and went without a gift a'tall."

Katie was quite certain she didn't have to worry about that happening. She and Dan had discussed the day just last week. No, her husband was altogether dependable. For sure and for certain.

◆

The next morning Katie slipped out of bed while it was still dark, tiptoeing downstairs to whip up Mary's lime salad, then slid it into the refrigerator. One less thing to do later. She was tempted to make the lemon sponge pie now but decided to wait. She didn't want Dan to notice the pie too early. Besides, if he was going over to visit Brother Miller this afternoon, she could bake it then. Same with the rest of the supper preparations.

Back upstairs she had a bath and was dressed before Dan's alarm clock jolted him awake. Turning the alarm off for him, she sat on the edge of his side of the bed, then leaned down and kissed him lightly on the cheek. "Wake up to our special day," she whispered.

His eyes fluttered, and he smiled up at her sleepily. "You're up and dressed . . . so soon?"

She nodded. "I had some things to tend to."

He sat up and stretched. "Happy day, Katie," he said, all smiles.

"Just think . . . we've been husband and wife for one year already."

He pulled her near and wrapped her in his arms. "Doesn't seem possible."

She thought back to all the months and years they'd been apart before their marriage, seemingly lost to each other. "What counts is that God put us together, jah?"

"We both know that to be true." With that, he smiled.

While Dan showered and dressed, Katie cooked up a batch of blueberry pancakes on the griddle and made her own pancake syrup using brown and white sugars, molasses, water, and maple flavoring. She let the mixture simmer, then removed it from the heat and added a little vanilla when she heard Dan's footsteps on the stairs. Homemade pancakes and syrup always put a smile on her beloved's face. Today was no exception.

"Well, what's this?" He'd spied the platter of blueberry pancakes. "Are we celebrating so early?" He went to her and slipped his arms around her waist, kissing the back of her neck.

"All day," she said.

They sat at the table, Dan saying nothing in return.

"It's all right with you, isn't it?" she asked quickly.

He looked at her with blank eyes. "What is?"

"That we celebrate for a full day?"

He smiled, nodding. "Sure, but you remember I'll be gone a good part of the afternoon."

The fact that he hadn't said a word about *his* plans made her wonder. But she wouldn't worry, not a bit. She bowed her head as Dan said the blessing over their food.

The morning's routine was similar to most every other Saturday. Dan got caught up in either answering the phone or making calls, so she spent the morning mending buttons on several of his dress shirts. Because he was caught up in his own doings, she had time to read a bit, even wrote a letter to a distant cousin over in Wisconsin.

The noon meal consisted of cold cuts, sliced cheeses, and freshly baked honey-oatmeal bread for sandwiches, pickled beets, and cottage cheese salad. Dan spoke of his work during the meal, showing enthusiasm for his company's plans for a new church building over near York. He also mentioned several small-group meetings, upcoming, where they'd been asked to play their guitars, things like that.

"Well, enough about me," he said. "How was the church bake sale?"

"A good amount of money came in for the mission fund."

"That's great. Any idea how much?"

She *had* known the tally, but that was yesterday and she'd already put it out of her mind. Her primary focus was on today. She longed to talk intimately about their life, their future together. A bit of romance, too, would be nice. "I've forgotten the amount" was all she said.

He pushed away from the table. "Thanks for a delicious meal, dear." He got up and pecked her on the forehead.

"*Gem gschehne*—you're welcome," Katie replied, wishing he might ask her to go with him on a walk or a drive somewhere.

"I'll see you at suppertime," he said later, heading off around two o'clock in the afternoon. "You don't mind, do you?"

She said she didn't. And she meant it; honestly, she did. It was just that she'd had such high expectations for the day. Hadn't known better, really, having never experienced a first wedding anniversary before. She hadn't witnessed her parents' first, of course, hadn't been to any of the People's first-wedding-anniversary dinners, not that she recalled, anyway. Well, she'd just make the best of it. Put on a stiff upper lip and hope the evening meal was a nice surprise, at least, for Daniel.

Meanwhile, she had more cooking and baking to do. But as the afternoon dragged on, the table set, steak simmering, lemon sponge pie waiting, she got to thinking if Dan might've forgotten to get her a present, just maybe. Could he have marked their date on the wrong calendar, like the husband whose wife had laughed about it yesterday at the bake sale?

Was it possible that Dan had simply failed to purchase a gift after all? Goodness knows how busy he'd been—they'd *both* been—all this week, what with the nightly meetings, Dan's busy work schedule, the church bake sale, not to mention her keeping up all the duties round the house. It was a wonder they weren't both reclining on the sofa, feet propped up on matching hassocks, too tired to talk or do much of anything else.

Fact was, she had boundless energy, and so, it seemed, did Dan. He'd been off doing who knows what at the Millers' for more than two hours now. It was coming up on four o'clock.

Along about quarter past four, here came Mamma driving horse and buggy into the lane, of all things. "Happy first wedding anniversary," her mother said, looking too serious. "Can't stay but a minute." Mamma carried a cardboard box with a pecan pie in it from Mary and a batch of homemade candy kisses and caramels. "Thought you might like something for your sweet tooth . . . and Dan's, too."

"Denki. So kind of you."

Their eyes locked and held at that moment, and Katie invited Mamma inside. "Dan's gone for a bit, but he'll be back in no time."

Mamma hesitated; a crooked little smile crossed her face. "Best be goin', really. Maybe some other time."

"All right, then." Katie took the box of goodies and thanked her mother again. "I'll tell Dan you stopped by."

"You do that," Mamma called over her shoulder, heading back toward the waiting carriage.

Katie stood at the back door, watching till the horse and carriage were out of sight. She turned and carried the box into the kitchen, taking out Mary's pecan pie first. They would enjoy it tomorrow noon, after church. Maybe she'd invite the Freys over for an afternoon visit, to share the pie.

Opening one of the caramels, she popped it into her mouth, not caring that the treat might take the edge off her appetite. It was nearly four-thirty now. What was keeping Dan?

She wanted to have candles lit and ice water poured in glasses, ready the minute her husband walked into the house. She found herself glancing out the front window, feeling far too uneasy. Still, she checked and double-checked her list and, after doing so several more times, decided she was perfectly ready.

When, at last, Dan pulled into the driveway just minutes after five o'clock, she scrambled away from the window, going to the dining room and striking a match to light the candles. Hastily, she poured cold water into the sparkling clean goblets.

A quick look around the table and she was satisfied. *Darlene was right . . . everything's fine.*

Dan greeted her warmly and washed his hands at the

kitchen sink, then went with her into the dining room. "Honey, this is so nice!" He turned and looked at her . . . *really* looked. "You've been working all afternoon, haven't you?"

"Wait'll you see what's for dessert," she said with a smile.

"Dessert? What about the first course?" His eyes shone with excitement as he sniffed the air. "I believe I smell steak."

She nodded, sitting down. "I hope you're hungry."

"Starved." He reached for her hand as he began to pray.

They took their time, enjoying the meal. Dan commented repeatedly on the tenderness and flavor of her Swiss steak, the tastiness of the creamed asparagus, too. He seemed delighted all round.

Katie was relieved that she had taken time to shine the windows, for she and Dan stared out as the day turned to dusk, watching birds in flight, seeing their Amish neighbor and his sons finishing up in the fields in the distance. They looked into each other's eyes, too, talking softly, laughing, having the best time. A long and leisurely meal, and Katie was only too glad to serve it.

She thought of presenting her gift to him during dessert, but then wondered how Dan might feel if he *hadn't* bought her something. No, she didn't want to embarrass him, nor put him on the spot. There was still plenty of time left in the day. She would wait.

"Mamma dropped by with some candies and a pie from Mary," she said.

Dan's eyes were wide. "Your mother was here?"

"I was a bit surprised myself."

"And . . . you said Mary, Bishop John's wife, sent over a pie?"

123

She knew what he was thinking. "Seems we're making progress."

He leaned back in his chair. "Well, I believe we are."

She wanted to say that they ought to continue praying for their families, for the People in general, but she struggled with a tiny lump in her throat. 'Specially when she served Dan his coffee and still nothing was said about his gift.

What shall I do? she wondered. *Dan will think I'm too eager.*

"Is everything all right?" he asked, while she offered him a sugar cube for his coffee.

"Why shouldn't it be?"

"You just seem . . . well, a bit sad."

This is silly, she told herself, not wanting to show her disappointment. Hadn't they, after all, had a lovely day together? What more was needed? They had each other, good conversation, delicious food.

"Would you care for more pie or . . . or anything?" she asked, her voice trembling.

"Katie . . . honey, what *is* it?" He took her hand in both of his.

"I, uh, just wondered when we should exchange our gifts to . . . to each other." The words came flying out, though she truly hadn't wanted to speak them at all. But, all the same, Dan gazed back at her, compassion shining from his eyes.

"Well, I didn't want to present my gift until I thought *you* were ready," he said, still holding her hand.

She should have known. They were in the same boat. He hadn't wanted to make her feel uncomfortable if she hadn't anything more to give him than the special meals and pie. *Bless his heart*, she thought, wanting to cry.

He excused himself to the front room, and she heard him talking on the phone. Soon he returned and said, "It won't be long now. The gift is on its way."

When the wagon came rattling into the lane, Dan had her cover her eyes. Then he led her gingerly to the back door. "Wait right here, Katie, and don't open your eyes till I say so."

She was ever so excited now as she waited for Dan's surprise. And she felt ashamed of herself, for thinking her darling had forgotten. Several minutes passed, and she wondered what was keeping him. Then he was at her side again, telling her, "You can look now."

When she opened her eyes, there was a lovely white porch swing down on the lawn. She ran out to see it up close. "Oh, Daniel . . . it's beautiful!"

"Do you like it?"

"Like it? It's exactly what I wished for." She sat down and tried out the swing, patting the seat next to her. "How on earth did you know?"

He sat beside her, grinning. "I'll never tell."

"It was Darlene, wasn't it?" She was in his arms, returning his kisses. "It's a wonderful-gut anniversary gift," she declared, spotting Brother Miller as he tipped his hat to her. So that's why Dan had been gone all afternoon.

Remembering the watch, she wiggled out of his embrace. "Wait right here," she said. "I have a gift for you, too."

Dashing upstairs, she headed straight for the clothes closet, to get the watchcase. She looked where she always kept secret gifts, but not finding it, thought she must've hidden the watch in one of her bureau drawers. She recalled that, on occasion, her mamma had often hidden things too well—so "safely" that they seemed to disappear, couldn't be found when needed. Where *had* she put Dan's gift? She thought hard, retracing her steps.

Then it dawned on her. She'd held the watchcase—the leather banded watch itself—in her hands, but downtown at the jewelry store. She had never purchased the gift at all. Too caught up with the preparations, the list-making, and other things, she had completely forgotten Dan's gift!

How could this be? She wept with the realization, dabbing at her wet cheeks as she flew back down the steps to apologize to her darling. "Ach, can you ever forgive me?" she choked out the words. "I followed my list so closely . . . but I forgot the most important thing!"

"Honey . . . honey," Dan said, reaching for her. "It's all right."

"No . . . no, I wanted to remember this day for as long as we live."

He stroked her hair, telling her all was well. "The day is not as important as our love, is it?" he whispered.

She hugged his neck, bemoaning the fact that she'd ordered his gift but failed to pick it up and told him so. "How could I have been so fuzzy-headed?"

"My darling girl," he said, a smile of forgiveness on his lips.

"Your gift will be waiting for you—here—the minute you get home on Monday," she promised.

During the remainder of the evening, Katie kept thinking of her inexcusable oversight, telling Dan how sorry and embarrassed she was. Next time, she might just forget about making a list at all. Truth was, it had thrown her off quite a bit. But more than that, she was determined not to be so quick to second-guess her dear husband in the future, on *any* account.

On Monday evening Katie presented Dan with the leather watch promptly as he came in the door. "Happy anniversary, darling . . . a little late."

He removed the ribbon and opened the box. Inspecting the watch, he traced the grain of the leather with his finger. A smile on his handsome face, he lifted the watch out of its case and placed it on his left wrist. "Now *this* is a gift worth waiting for!"

"A gift to remember," she said. "To be sure."

He reached for her, and they tumbled into each other's arms, having such a hearty good laugh.

PART II

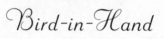

Bird-in-Hand

There was the grace of swaying willows, the
tranquility of clear, chirping brooks, the honesty of
wide-open skies, and the blessing and abundant
love of the People.

—from *The Postcard*

$\mathcal{F}$riend to $\mathcal{F}$riend

That their hearts might be comforted, being knit together in love. . . .
—Colossians 2:2

Rachel Bradley stood on the front porch, looking out across the wide yard to the broad pastureland, a gentle afternoon shower under way. All morning she'd pondered her recent letter from Esther Glick, out in Holmes County, Ohio. Seemed her dear cousin had her hands mighty full with newborn triplets, the third baby comin' as a big surprise, seein' as how the doctor had said all along *twins*.

She could read between the lines, no getting round that. Rachel knew Esther well enough to sense a prevailing melancholy tone—the unspoken quality to *this* letter from her usually cheerful cousin. Remembering her own "baby blues" after the births of her children, most recently a nine-pound baby boy born over a year ago, Rachel thought long and hard 'bout what she might write back as encouragement. From one young mother's heart to another.

"Dear Lord, what would ya have me write to Esther?" A sudden clap of thunder sent her scurrying for the house. Once inside, she checked on her napping toddler, then settled down at the kitchen table. Pen in hand, she began to write on her best stationery.

Dearest Cousin Esther,

Greetings in the precious name of our Lord and Savior Jesus Christ.

You can't possibly know how happy I was to get your letter this morning. Ach, it was ever so gut to hear from you, really 'twas. Even though I have plenty of friends here in Bird-in-Hand—sisters and cousins, and whatnot—nothing takes the place of a bosom buddy. I can't count the times you've lifted my spirits with a Scripture verse or two . . . and your fervent prayers for me. I'm ever so grateful, Esther. You mean so much to me, knowin' how you put your trust one hundred percent in our Lord Jesus.

Well, seems to me you may be suffering some these days— prob'ly a bit run down, and tired, too—what with the birth of your wee sons and daughter. Three babies. My, oh my, you must surely be wondering what our heavenly Father was a-thinkin'. But never forget that God knew what He was doing, sending you and Levi three children all at once. You can surely put your faith and trust in that.

I'm glad to hear you've got yourself several extra pairs of hands from the community helpin' out. How I wish we lived as neighbors to you and Levi. You know I'd be over every morning, and what fun we'd have changing and dressing one baby after another. Must seem mind-bogglin' for you, every so often, but I know you're a wonderful-gut mother, Esther, and these early days won't last forever. Try and take one day as it comes, all right? Surely, you don't expect to keep the house neat as a pin just now. Nobody there thinks any differently,

I'm sure. (If they do, best put 'em to work mopping and cleaning, why don'tcha?)

Remember, we're only a prayer apart.

Rachel put down her pen for a moment. She wondered if Esther's mamma was plannin' to make the trip out to Ohio. Hadn't heard a word 'bout it from anyone. Knowing Esther as she did, her cousin wouldn't press the issue, wouldn't come right out and ask her mother to come. But for Esther's sake and her new babes in arms, Rachel hoped Aunt Leah would find it in her heart to indeed go.

I've been thinking 'bout giving your mamma a call—encourage her, you know. I'm praying 'bout this, you can be sure. It's time the gap is breached, I should say. 'Tis past time.

She wouldn't go on and on 'bout the thorny problem, the wedge that had come between Esther and her mamma. No, best to trust the Lord on such matters.

Rachel continued writing.

It's hard even for me to believe it, but Annie's in the second grade this year already. Reads fairly well, I must say, and she's right happy 'bout printing her own name, as well as her new baby brother's. Every day she comes home all smiles, eager to show her pop and me the lessons she's learning. Philip went down to the neighborhood general store and bought a tiny chalkboard, just big enough for her to write her numbers on. ABC's too.

Ach, you'd be surprised at how my Philip's takin' to fatherhood—to the whole of the Amish community, too. So good, he is, with our little Gabriel. Likes to sit out in the yard with both Annie and Gabe of an evening, soakin' up the things in nature that attracted him here in the first place, I s'pose. Things like an abandoned bird's nest, a garden path strewn with scarlet leaves, and lightning bugs. Why, sometimes, it seems as if he's seein' things through the eyes of Annie and our baby son.

Philip says he's learned more from the children—'bout the pleasure of nature—than the other way round. Creek beds and apple orchards are all places where wonder begins. We need only to join our children, get right down on our hands and knees, in order to see the miracle of God's creation. Jah, our youngsters teach us ever so much, ain't?

My husband is forever sharin' with me bits and pieces of his former life in New York. Says it's just too easy in the modern-day culture to lose touch with nature. English folk don't seem to have much time for the natural world, even though we're all made by God to hunger after the earth and sky. So . . . nature's rhythms get lost in the shuffle of livin', and how sad 'tis.

For me, I can't imagine marchin' to another beat—the drumbeat of the city—spending day after day inside, breathing secondhand air, awash in artificial white lights, bounded by concrete and glass and whatnot all.

"Any relationship demands time and plenty of it," says Philip. I'm a-thinkin' he's feelin' the loss, having missed out on a connection with nature, so to speak, by growing up in a big city, by not playing heartily as Amish youngsters do (when chores are caught up)—in the dirt, makin' mud pies, splashin' through streams, gatherin' up stones and shells, and occasionally catchin' bullheads out in the pond. Outdoors is where a body can let thoughts wander to high heavens. But, then, I'm not telling you anything new.

Well, things are wonderful-gut here with my dear husband by my side. He's happy as a lark, I do believe, working the land by day, writin' his stories by night. He wears the black broad fall trousers I sew for him—tan suspenders, too—'specially on the days he works alongside our Old Order neighbors up the road apiece. With his full beard, I daresay Philip looks as Plain as any of the rest of us.

So, a cheerful foursome, we are. Isn't God good to bring such joy to this former widow's heart?

Best be thinking 'bout supper here perty soon. Before I sign off, though, here are two Scriptures that've kept me goin' myself a number of times: Philippians 4:7 and 13. "And the peace of God, which passeth all understanding, shall keep your hearts and minds through Christ Jesus." And, "I can do all things through Christ which strengtheneth me."

May the Lord bless and keep you always in His care, Esther. Please give your baby trio a hug and kiss from their cousin in Lancaster County . . . the older children, too.

Love always,
Rachel

She set about preparing supper, peeling potatoes and putting a thawed ham in the oven. That done, she dialed Aunt Leah's telephone number. "Well, how's the new grandmammi?" Rachel said after exchanging greetings.

"Oh my . . . three at once," came the reply. "Can you imagine?"

She couldn't, not at all, but didn't say so. "Sounds to me like Esther's head-over-heels in babies."

"Surely she's got herself some extra help. She'd *have* to."

"Folks from the church is all I know." She wondered if Aunt Leah might take the hint, think of giving Esther a hand.

"'Spect Levi's more of a hinder than a help, the babies bein' so tiny 'n' all."

She didn't know 'bout that. Levi was prob'ly a right gut father, far as Rachel knew.

"I've been thinkin' things over," Aunt Leah said, out of the blue. "Thought I just might hire me a driver and make a trip out there, help my daughter with her babies."

Rachel was ever so relieved. For too long there'd been a rift between Esther and her parents, 'specially after Levi Glick decided to up and leave Lancaster County, taking his wife and young family along. Other things, too—certain church teachings—had gotten in the way of the tie that binds for the past few years.

"I'd say your going oughta cheer Esther up. Fact is, I *know* it will," Rachel replied.

"Oh? Is Esther blue, then?"

"Well . . . a little, jah." She wouldn't reveal too much.

"Ach, I'm awful glad you said so, 'cause I know just what she needs." Aunt Leah seemed eager to talk all of a sudden. "I'll take along some catnip tea, that and raspberry tea. Both'll perk her up a bit, help her sleep better at night, I 'spect. She'll feel gut as new."

"Hadn't thought of it, but, jah, such a gut idea."

There was a slight pause. Then Aunt Leah said, "You and Esther seem to see eye to eye, ain't so?"

Rachel didn't quite know what to say. "We're cousins by birth, friends by choice." She might've said, "And sisters in the Lord, because of Calvary's cross," but let it go at that.

"Esther, she's in need of close friends, way out there so far from home and all," Aunt Leah remarked, her voice a bit forced now.

Rachel agreed. "I would think she'd get homesick, jah."

"Why they ever left, I'll never know. . . ."

Truth was, Aunt Leah *did* know. Her son-in-law was a-hankerin' for land. There was plenty of it to go around farther west.

Rachel sighed. "Well, I mustn't keep you, Aunt Leah. The Lord bless you and give you a safe trip . . . and a right good time in Holmes County."

Another pause, then—"You say you're still close with my Esther?"

"Oh my, yes, ever so close." Rachel could've gone on and on, tellin' her aunt just how dear her Ohio cousin was to her, but Aunt Leah should know that. "Esther and I . . . well, I daresay, we're just like you and Mamma. Close as sisters."

Aunt Leah said no more.

"I wrote her a letter. Thought I'd mail it off tomorrow," Rachel said quickly, thinking she oughta bring the conversation to an end.

"Why don't I deliver it in person for you?"

"Wonderful-gut," Rachel replied. "Denki—thanks."

"One gut turn deserves another."

Rachel had to smile as she said good-bye and hung up the phone. Hurrying off to check on her own little one, she couldn't help but think that just maybe things were starting to move in a new direction for Esther and her mamma. 'Course, then, only time would tell.

Thinkin' on it even more, Rachel wondered, too, if the Lord might've blessed Aunt Leah with triplet grandbabies as a way of healing the families. Just maybe 'twas.

Raising Zook's Barn

*Let us do good unto all men, especially unto them who are
of the household of faith.*

—Galatians 6:10

Philip Bradley, former New York journalist, had lived
most of his life far from the fold of the People. Marrying Rachel Yoder, a beautiful Amish widow, had been the best choice
he'd ever made for himself. That, and embracing wholeheartedly the conservative customs of the New Order Amish
church.

Promptly, he had abandoned his fashionable attire, tech-
nological conveniences, and even his car, although he kept it
in good repair parked behind the house for dire emergencies.
He had voluntarily grown a beard—without a mustache, as
was Amish custom—donned the traditional clothing of the
brethren, and "unplugged" his freelance writing—a big adjust-
ment in and of itself.

Another challenge was keeping Rachel's relatives' names
straight in his mind, his in-laws as numerous as the sands of
the sea. They consisted of nearly two hundred folk, counting

Rachel's parents, her aunts, uncles, grandparents, first cousins, and their spouses and children. Remembering which Amos Esh or John Zook was married to which Mary Esh or Rebecca Zook was a significant feat. The People recycled their first names, frequently intermarrying, creating the obstacle of re-calling both first *and* last names for the newcomer and former outsider. Which—he would have been naïve to think other-wise—was how some of the People still viewed him.

Even after two years of wholly following the Lord and working the soil, he wondered if some of the brethren might still be talking among themselves. *Does Philip have staying power? Will he eventually throw in the towel, abandon the rigors of Plain life?* they might ask, though discreetly. Especially one such soul.

Moses Raber.

The exceptionally tall, middle-aged carpenter had a way of showing up when Philip least expected, overly scrutinizing, observing him.

To set the record straight, Philip had not entertained thoughts of leaving the community, not once he'd vowed "to love and to cherish" Rachel, promising to raise her daughter, Annie, and now his own toddler, Gabriel, "in the fear and admonition of the Lord." His new family was his very life, his purpose for living. God had picked up the pieces of his wan-dering soul, set him on a straight and narrow path, given him an unmistakable spring in his step. But, no matter the power of his original decision to unite with the People, the process had been far more difficult than he might have first thought upon falling in love with Rachel . . . and this tranquil piece of God's green earth.

He had been fitting in fairly well, or at least he thought so, until the day John Zook's barn was hit by lightning. After that, things went directly south in a New York minute.

Philip had been helping fill Rachel's great-uncle Amos Yoder's silo. A whole group of men were on hand, since Uncle Amos had suffered a fall a few days before and was laid up in bed with a bad hip, being nursed back to health by his faithful wife, Becky Ann.

The afternoon was balmy; the sweet scent of ripening apples hung in the air like the tantalizing promise of dessert after a meal. The men worked hard and fast, each with his straw hat secured on his head, hoping to beat the rains. ("Severe thunderstorms," the newspaper had forecast.)

"Looks like a storm a-brewin'," Jacob Stoltzfus said, removing his hat and wiping his brow. Jacob was one of several Amish farmers helping fill the silo.

Pausing in his work, Philip noticed black clouds building in the northeast. "Maybe we should call it a day," he suggested.

"Jah, best be headin' home," another farmer said. The others nodded silently.

"Tomorrow we'll work again . . . bright and early." Jacob frowned at the angry sky.

"*Da Herr sei mit du*—the Lord be with you," Philip called as the men headed to the barn to hitch up their horses to parked buggies. On foot as usual, he hadn't learned to drive a horse-drawn buggy.

"Care for a ride?" Jacob asked while hitching up his horse.

"I'll walk this time . . . thanks anyway." At the end of the lane, he headed north toward Lavina Troyer's sprawling farmhouse, where he and Rachel lived with their growing family in the larger main section. Lavina had been so kind to offer the residence, apparently more than ready to have the newlyweds move into her side of the house. She promptly moved to the smaller addition—the Dawdi Haus—where she now lived and cared for Adele Herr, their aging English friend, who had ties to the People.

◆

When the first bolt of lightning triggered a *snap*, Philip was walking on the treelined road, headed for home. After a few more near misses, he decided to take cover in a nearby tobacco shed at the home of neighbors Amos and Rose Mary Beiler.

Safe inside, he peered out between the boards in the shed. Jagged, unpredictable voltage plunged from the dark sky like the hand of God. A powerful wind came up, bending small trees and spinning windmills. Rachel, he knew, would be anxious for his return, so he crept out of the shed and sprinted the rest of the way, praying for God's protection as one bolt of lightning after another zapped the ground.

Rachel was waiting at the back door, just as he expected. "Ach, 's'good to see my husband in one piece," she greeted him.

Kissing her cheek, he assured her—while in his strong embrace—that he was all right. "We don't have lightning like this in New York," he joked, going into the kitchen.

"Awful close, was it?"

Nodding, he engaged in a bit of small talk, then headed up

the steps to change clothes. At the landing, he stopped and leaned over the banister. "Do I have time to shower before supper?" he asked.

She said he did. And at that instant a powerful lightning bolt burst to the ground outside the living room window, followed by an ear-piercing crack of thunder that shook the house. Annie shrieked with fright downstairs, and young Gabe began to howl.

Within minutes the loud dinner bell started ringing at John Zook's farm, their neighbor to the south. It continued to toll, indicating an emergency. "Lightning must've hit the barn," Philip told Rachel.

"I hope it's not the house," said Rachel, a concerned look on her pretty face. "Prob'ly it's the barn on fire. If so, they'll need help getting cattle and equipment out. Best go 'n' help save as much as possible."

Having never assisted in a fire, Philip had no idea what he was getting into. He made a dash across the open field that led to Zook's dairy farm. Surveying the menacing sky, he hoped for rain. *God has natural ways of putting out fires,* he thought. But as he ran he saw in the near distance the ropes of smoke beginning to ascend heavenward as orange flames licked at the barn roof.

He rushed to the barnyard. A handful of Amish farmers had already responded to the continual ringing of the dinner bell; some of them were coming up the lane on mules, others on horseback, the fastest way to arrive.

"Help us get the cows out!" Zook's wife and daughters called, waving their arms.

He and several other men ran into the barn, holding their

breath against stinging smoke, untying one cow after another. The animals loped out of the barn door, heading toward the pasture, bawling loudly. Mules and draught horses were next.

Zook's teenage sons and a growing army of men grabbed whatever small pieces of barn equipment they could salvage, dragging them away from the flames. Zook's youngest son continued ringing the bell, summoning even more Amish neighbors. A dozen or more came on foot. Already, there were three men on the roof, a precarious spot, Philip thought, though no one showed any alarm as buckets of water were hoisted up by rope. On the ground, old Grandfather Zook shouted commands, as though he'd witnessed a number of barn burnings, knowing precisely what to do.

"Has anyone called the fire department?" asked Philip, working feverishly with the others. Power hoses could douse a fire of this magnitude in no time.

Moses Raber shot him a severe look. "Phones are all out . . . up and down the road."

"Lightning took out the Englischers' phone lines," said another farmer.

By now one whole side of the barn leaned dangerously, tilting toward the center. If fire trucks didn't come in short order, Zook's barn would collapse.

Philip hauled an armful of small hand tools out of the barn and dropped them on the lawn. That's when he spotted a blue pickup parked near the house. Dashing across the barnyard, he looked inside the small truck. The keys were hanging in the ignition! He looked around, trying to determine who the owner might be, to ask permission to drive to the fire station.

He saw only Amishmen. And the gaping hole in the barn's

side. He felt the heat, too, and the pitiful whinny screams of a stray mule. The farmers' jaws were rigid in their determination, fighting a losing battle. Zook's enormous barn was being eaten alive by an unbeatable blaze.

Without thinking, Philip jumped into the pickup and started the engine. "I'll get help!" he shouted to no one in particular.

Moses Raber heard and cast a glaring eye his way.

Philip backed up the pickup, then headed down the lane and out to the road. He sped to Route 340, turning west at the junction, toward the fire station.

En route back to Zook's farm, the fire truck wailed its boisterous siren. Red lights flashed, alerting motorists as it screamed down the highway. Philip followed close behind in the borrowed pickup.

At the intersection, the fire truck ran the red light. Philip, not trailing through, was stopped momentarily. Waiting for the light to change, he happened to glance over at the car on his right. The driver and a carload of passengers were gawking and pointing at him.

The fire siren had certainly called attention to him—an *Amishman* driving a pickup truck! Groaning, he realized what a spectacle he was, with straw hat and cropped hair, behind the wheel of the sleek blue pickup. A reporter's heyday. And he should know, having chased hundreds of sensational stories over the years.

Attempting to ignore the ridicule coming from the car, he found himself impatient for the green light. When the light turned, he stomped on the gas pedal.

But the mocking driver trailed too close to his bumper, following him down the long road to Zook's lane. The car scarcely slowed, swerving around him, just as he made the turnoff. "Stick with a horse and buggy, why don'tcha!" the driver hollered, laying on the horn and making a general ruckus. The car sped on, dust clouds billowing up.

Chagrined, Philip drove toward the house and parked the pickup exactly where he had found it, leaving the keys in the ignition once again. The firefighters were already using the hoses, combating the flames. He ran to watch, hoping against hope the barn, or a portion of it, might be spared.

After a time Zook himself seemed to give up hope. The farmer came and stood near Philip, face smudged, his thick brown hair now gray with soot. "There was just no savin' it . . . no matter." Zook shook his head solemnly. "An act of God."

After the firefighters left the scene, the men scattered out to survey the charred timbers, though from a safe distance. Smoldering blue-black smoke continued to billow high into the sky. "We did all we could," Jacob Stoltzfus said finally.

"Jah," agreed John Zook, glancing back at Philip. "That, we did."

" 'Twas the wrath of God on this community of believers," another farmer said gravely.

Moses eyed Philip critically, as if to point a finger. Was he judging Philip, questioning whether or not the outsider's life measured up?

Many Old Order church members believed that such an

act by the Almighty, which destroyed a staunch member's property, signified divine wrath on the entire group. Consequently, each person in that church district was morally bound to offer assistance to the hapless neighbor.

Jacob called out loudly from the crowd, "We're our brother's keeper. We'll raise a fine barn for John Zook." At the mention of reconstruction, the men nodded in agreement.

In the midst of all the talk, a stocky dark-haired man came out of the crowd and sauntered over to Philip. "Was it *you* who drove my pickup?" he demanded.

Recognizing the man as Vern Eisenberger, a feed salesman, Philip replied, "I see that it may have been a mistake. I only borrowed your pickup for—"

"You *borrowed* without asking, which in my book is stealing." Vern was breathing fast, eyes wide. "What sort of Amishman drives anyway... takes a truck that doesn't belong to him?" His scowl grew more severe. "How is it you can work a clutch . . . unless maybe you stripped it but good?"

Philip considered telling Vern that he'd owned a number of vehicles—standard shift and automatic alike. None of that was relevant now.

John Zook's youngest son spoke up. "Philip was only tryin' to spare Pop's barn."

"Jah, and he almost did, too," said the boy's friend. "Didn'tcha see them firefighters goin' after it? Come near to salvaging at least some of the big timbers."

Just then Moses came and stood shoulder to shoulder with Vern, as if choosing sides. "You wanna know what sort of Amishman takes things into his own hands?" he retorted. "I'll tell ya who!"

Moses was stopped, if momentarily, by Zook himself, who came rushing over with several others. "Just what's goin' on here?" John eyed both Vern and Moses.

Vern bellowed, "One of your church members walked off with my pickup." He pointed an accusing finger at Philip before turning to inspect the truck's exterior.

"Well, now, he returned it, didn't he?" John insisted.

Moses shot back, gray eyes flashing, "Philip shouldn't have driven at all, according to our ways."

Philip was embarrassed. By acting impulsively, he had put himself—the whole group—at risk for ridicule. Everything he had endeavored to be, all that he wanted to do in this community of friends and neighbors—was it now in jeopardy because of one careless deed?

Moses continued to rant and rave, asking Philip point-blank if he had a license to drive and if not, said, "You're breakin' the laws of God *and* man both. Too worldly, you are!"

At that declaration, John slipped his arm into the crook of the taller man's elbow, leading Moses to one side of the house.

The feed salesman tapped the hood of his pickup. "Good thing there aren't any nicks or scratches." He opened the door on the driver's side, slamming it shut. The engine roared to life, and he backed up too fast, swaying from one side of the narrow lane to the other, then spun recklessly back onto the dirt road at the end of Zook's lane, tires squealing as he went.

"Mad as a hornet," Philip muttered.

" 'Tis no need for anger such as that," said Jacob Stoltzfus, gripping his straw hat in front of him.

"Jah, no need," echoed Zook's youngest boy. The lad turned, looking toward his father and Moses, who were still talking heatedly beside the house.

"I'll tell ya why Vern's fumin'," Zook's oldest son spoke up. "Pop was out in the field, telling Vern that he'd thought it over and decided to change to a different brand of feed . . . just minutes before the lightning hit."

"That explains the tiff," Philip said, wondering what was causing Moses to be so disturbed. He went around talking with the men gathered there, several individually, others in groups, explaining his motive for driving the pickup. They assured him there was no ill will. But by the way Moses was behaving, waving his arms and raising his voice, Philip knew he had offended at least one of the brethren.

"We learn from mistakes and try not to repeat 'em," said a stout farmer, a deep frown on his brow.

"When it comes to fellas like Vern Eisenberger," said Jacob Stoltzfus, "it's best to be on the safe side and not offend."

"Ain't such a good testimony," said another.

"Just remember, Vern's bark is worse than his bite," said Jacob, his hand on Philip's shoulder. "Be in prayer for him."

Feeling only slightly encouraged, Philip headed down the road, going home for the second time in a day.

At supper Philip described for Rachel what had transpired at Zook's farm. She didn't seem to be surprised at the feed salesman's reaction. "Vern wouldn't be any too happy 'bout losing a customer, that's for sure." She said Mr. Eisenberger was "prob'ly ripe for an outburst. You just so happened to get in his way—bore the brunt of his anger."

"I hope nothing more comes of this." Philip knew he must abide by the unspoken rules of the People, at all costs. Follow more carefully the example of the other men, particularly those established in the faith. Ignore his impulsive instincts. And, as best as he could, try to steer clear of Moses Raber, who was downright rude for an Amishman—truly a rarity in this community.

Philip wasn't deceiving himself; he did not comprehend everything in the society of the Plain or the way certain things were done or expected to be handled on occasion. But understanding fully had never been part of what had drawn him here in the first place.

He went to his knees in prayer in the quietude of the front room, asking the Lord first for forgiveness in the matter, and secondly, for wisdom and grace in further dealings he might have with the irate feed salesman—and Moses Raber.

———◆———

The next day, thanks to the blessing of intense rains in the night, Zook hired heavy equipment to be used in raking out the embers beneath the scorched partial skeleton of their barn, silhouetted against a brilliant sky. Hordes of neighboring farmers came with wheelbarrows and shovels to help clean up and, later, to assess the damage, several of them commenting on other fires in the Lancaster area. That was the talk of the day—the frequency of fires, especially in hot summer months when lightning strikes accounted for most of the damage to barns.

A barn, after all, was a thing to be revered. A safe haven for animals—cows, mules, sometimes goats—and a place to store hay during the winter months, as well as keep farm equipment and tools in an orderly manner. The barn was also a place where courtship rituals were encouraged and kept alive, the location of Sunday night singings, where Amish teenagers met to fellowship, sing, and pair off for the ride home.

In most cases a good, solid barn was built first, even before the farmhouse. The Amish saying that "a good barn built made many a fine house" wasn't just an old adage; it stood for a life philosophy.

Jacob Stoltzfus stared at the spot where Zook's barn had been. "Time we start planning a frolic," he said, his voice grave but firm. "We'll have us a new barn in a week or so."

The other men, wide-brimmed straw hats grasped securely in hand, nodded soberly. And two days later, Obadiah King, the master barn builder, arrived in his old gray buggy to step out the new barn's borders. Obadiah paced off the area several times, then stopped to drum his fists on the charred beams, to see if any might be utilized. A post-framed barn was already in the works—in Obadiah's head.

"He's raised many a barn," Zook's wife, Rebecca, said. "Doesn't even need a blueprint. Now, how 'bout that?"

"Jah, it's all up here," said Zook's oldest son, pointing to his own head.

So there would be mortise-and-tenon joints fastened by hickory pegs, an old system of construction, but one that would yield a most solid barn. The People's way.

"What do you know about barn raisings?" Philip asked Rachel after supper.

Before she could speak, young Annie, blond and blue-eyed, had an answer for him. "Ach, frolics are ever so much fun, Pop. You'll see."

"Now . . . now," Rachel gently scolded the youngster, "you must surely be thinking 'bout all the playin' that goes on in the corncrib with the other children, and pulling the wagon round with your wee cousins, and whatnot." Then, turning to Philip, she said, smiling, "Barn raisings make for a long and busy day. Backbreakin' work for the men, for sure and for certain, but Obadiah gives each of the men a particular duty, so no one's left out."

That's what Philip wanted to know, whether or not he would be assigned a specific task. "According to a person's skills?" he asked.

Rachel nodded, eyes bright. "Jah, Obadiah will team you up with a more experienced worker, prob'ly an older man. You'll use your muscles; he'll use his brain. But Obadiah will know best."

How the elder man had any clue as to Philip's abilities, he didn't know, but evidently word gets around in the community. People talk.

He reminded Rachel of his transgression, having taken the feed salesman's pickup without the owner's consent. "You made things right, though, jah?" she asked, waving her hand, then advising him to "keep workin' on your Amish awareness . . . the Plain consciousness, so to speak."

Made things right . . . Had he, really? No, he had not apologized to Vern Eisenberger that day.

His mind wandered back to all the things he'd readily given up to become Plain. Computer, printer, scanner, fax line, e-mail—the works. Even writing articles and his short-story anthology by long hand. Each evening, after their family time of reading the Bible and praying together, Philip often wrote at his antique rolltop desk, while Rachel happily kept him company as she crocheted or rocked little Gabe to sleep. The nineteenth-century tambour desk had been one of his smartest purchases—that and an electric typewriter for completed and revised manuscripts to be sent off to various editors. Shedding his computer initially had been a step in the right direction, especially when inquiries of his "work" came up among Plain friends. Invariably, the question of his livelihood—what he did to make a living, aside from farming work—somehow entered their dialogue. When he mentioned that he was a writer, there seemed to be fewer eyebrows raised if he quickly explained that he used pen and paper. Although, the writing life wasn't something too many Amish understood. A fascination—even obsession—with the arrangement and rearrangement of words was typically not understood among the general public, either.

Some of his Plain friends may have suspected him of keeping a journal about their activities, making use of his newfound "faith" as a means of exploitation. But he'd never considered that, hadn't even thought of publishing his most recent stories. Not until Rachel read one of them and insisted that he send it off to an editor. He'd asked her why she thought it so important, and her response had been emphatic. "It's time the English read some truth 'bout us. Such a lot of myths, there are—things made up. It'd be awful nice to see something in print that's *waahrhaft*—truthful."

He'd smiled at her insistence, gathering her into his arms, holding her near, this lovely woman who believed in him. "I'll think it over" was all he said. Now he again considered Rachel's idea, especially since Zook's barn burned down. "What about a story featuring a barn raising?" he asked his wife.

"I don't see why not," came her enthusiastic reply. "Plenty a' folks outside our community prob'ly have no idea what goes into such a task."

"What if I told on myself, in the story, that my behavior had caused a disagreement among the brethren? Show our humanity . . . that we're not perfect as some may think."

Rachel liked the idea. So he continued writing, with the Lancaster farmland as a backdrop to his narrative, enjoying every minute. He would not concern himself with deciding which of his magazine publishers was the right one. Not until the final draft was approved by Rachel.

Candidly, he shared the joys, the blunders, and even the laughable things that had happened to him since "joining church," as the People said. But he was cognizant of his most recent gaffe.

"The brethren don't hold grudges, do they?" he asked Rachel as they talked softly in bed one night.

Her pleasant countenance turned to a frown. "Why wouldja think so, dear?"

"Moses is aloof every time I come in contact with him.

154

Especially since Zook's barn fire."

She reached for his hand. "Moses is Old Order, remember. Don't worry yourself. The last thing he prob'ly wants to see is a fancy seeker comin' into the neighborhood and surprising everyone by staying put for a lifetime." Rachel paused, a smile on her face now. Then she grew more thoughtful. "Besides, I'm thinkin' all the men must surely realize by now you grew up differently."

"I've certainly made my share of mistakes since coming here," Philip said.

Rachel leaned her head on his shoulder. "Are you thinkin' of the day you rode in Ezra Lapp's buggy?"

He hadn't thought of that particular day recently. But since his sweetheart had reminded him of the incident, he definitely wanted to include the account in his ever-growing story collection. . . .

It was entirely by accident that he had accepted a ride in Ezra Lapp's carriage. Late in the afternoon, walking home from helping a neighboring farmer harvest corn, Philip noticed Ezra and son Amos driving toward him. "Wanna lift?" Ezra had asked.

"Well, sure. Denki," he'd said, hopping into the backseat.

"We've gotta make one stop on the way," Ezra added. "Hope it's not a bother."

"Fine with me." And he settled back, watching the autumn scenery go by, listening as the father and son talked. His ears perked up when they switched to *Deitsch*—Pennsylvania Dutch—the German dialect spoken by Amish, not a written language. The Lapps were most likely unaware that he understood some of the unique language, due to Rachel's and Annie's ongoing instruction. "Deitsch is our home language . . .'tis ever so soothing," Rachel had told him, explaining that most Amish children speak it almost exclusively until the final year before they attend first grade.

So the Lapps continued to converse with each other in Dutch, discussing such topics as hopping a bus ("goin' to Washington to witness the inauguration, if'n George W. Bush gets voted in as President"), also which young couples they suspected of courting and heading for marriage come November's wedding season.

Philip listened with interest, finding the men's curiosity at going to the nation's capital "to see history made before our eyes" most intriguing. "I thought we Plain folk steered clear of politics," he said suddenly, forgetting that the Lapps might not have realized he understood Dutch.

"Well, I declare . . ." Ezra turned around and grinned.

"You pick up quick-like," said Amos.

"Sorry, I didn't mean to eavesdrop."

"Jah, I believe you did!" Ezra replied, still beaming from ear to ear.

They had a good laugh over it, but when Philip tried to get back to his question about politics they'd arrived at the blacksmith's—their only stop—and both men jumped out of the carriage, leaving him alone, the reins for the horse draped loosely over the front of the buggy.

Thinking he might move up one seat, at least hold the reins and sit in front, lest the horse wander off down the road with an inexperienced Amishman at the helm, he quickly crawled over the seat and sat there. He picked up the reins and, without warning, the horse began to trot.

"Whoa!" he called, hoping not to frighten the animal further. Yet the horse continued on.

Then, out on the road, the thirteen-hundred-pound thoroughbred began to gallop, making a sharp right at the traffic light at Highway 340, heading west toward the city of Lancaster.

"Whoa!" Philip shouted again, pulling back hard on the reins. "Stop!" But the horse paid no attention. Drivers of cars took notice, though, quickly turning off the road, blaring horns, making matters worse. "Lord, help me!" Philip prayed loudly, now standing in the carriage as he continued to jerk on the bridle.

Obviously upset—out of control—the horse ran toward a mailbox, the buggy sideswiping a fence in the process. After the collision, the carriage slid to the left and spun around, while the horse twisted free, dragging forty-some pounds of harness apparatus behind as he sped on, heading south on Lynwood Road.

Meanwhile, Philip found himself sprawled under the Lapps' buggy, grateful he hadn't been injured but puzzled by what to do about the liberated horse.

In the end, both he and the horse made news headlines. Lapp's steed traveled nearly to Strasburg on Route 896, coming to a halt in front of Eldreth Pottery, in the parking lot. Sweating profusely, the animal's hind legs were gouged and bleeding from the constant rubbing of hitch and straps of the harness. . . .

"I should've remained sitting in the second seat." Philip

could chuckle *now* as he caressed Rachel's long hair. "Hind-sight is far better than foresight."

She laughed softly. "Who would've thought Dobbin might carry on so?"

He knew he needed lessons in driving a horse-drawn carriage. Thankfully, Lapp hadn't held him responsible, and he'd tried to make it up to the farmer by helping with harvest that year, without pay. Ezra, though, wouldn't hear of it.

Rachel wasn't at all surprised when she heard of Philip's attempt to make restitution. "People don't usually hold grudges round here . . . not for something as innocent as that."

The event had brought plenty of laughs among the farmers; not at his expense, though he knew they thought of him as a novice. "We only laugh *with* you, Philip," his father-in-law, Benjamin Zook, liked to remind him. "Never *at* you."

"Didja ever find out what Ezra Lapp meant by wantin' to go to the inauguration?" asked Rachel sleepily.

He wondered if he ought to say. Fact was, both Ezra, his son, and another Amishman from nearby Gordonville were hoping to go. But only if Bush was the new man in office. They had high hopes that George W. might restore principles of honesty and respectability to America. "Our country deserves that," Ezra had said recently. He also hoped for a better standard of farm commodity prices. Too many farmers had quit over the past twenty-four years or so. Several thousand acres had been thrown out of production. A sad state of affairs.

Ezra had given Philip the tip that the Gordonville farmer planned to keep a diary of the trip, if they went. "Go on over and talk to him. See if he'll discuss politics with you," joked Ezra.

But Philip had dropped the issue. No need to seek out someone—risk annoyance—for the sake of a good story. He would wait for election results, then see which farmers actually followed through with the Washington trip.

He left Rachel the next morning and went on foot to John Zook's, deep in thought. He had read accounts of outsiders—called "seekers" by mainstay Amish—who'd joined various conservative sects. And there always seemed to be a small frac-tion of folk from the "old school" who eyed a newcomer with suspicion, even skepticism. He had heard over the past few days—through the grapevine, unreliable as it was—that Moses was saying things like "Philip must be tryin' to enter the sheepfold another way, his driving Vern's pickup . . . keeping a car out behind the house and whatnot."

Grieved by the accusation, Philip had gone to visit his and Rachel's New Order pastor, getting their minister's opinion on the matter. In the end, Philip had asked for prayer, "for divine guidance in my dealings with Moses," he said.

The pastor suggested Philip pay John Zook a visit soon. A long-standing and devout member of the Old Order Amish, John was known to be slow to speak and quick to forgive. So Philip went to make things right, since the transgression had occurred on John's property . . . and Zook himself had been witness to the anger from both Vern and Moses.

John was at work in the small woodshed behind the chicken house when Philip arrived. The workshop door was standing open. Stooping, Philip poked his head in the doorway and saw John leaning against the workbench, holding a mug of black coffee.

"Morning."

He looked up. "*Wie gehts*, Philip."

"Thought I'd come over and talk." He wondered if John had heard the buzz going around. Moving to the workbench, he picked up some wood shavings and stared at them in his hand.

"What's on your mind?"

"Word has it I'm a troublemaker."

John shook his head. "Moses talks too much . . . always has."

"He watches me like a hawk."

"Never mind 'bout Moses. You made a poor judgment call, nothing more," John said with a slow smile.

"I'm sorry about that." Philip let the wood shavings fall onto the workbench. "There's something else." The feed salesman kept coming to mind. Philip wanted to clear the air with John while he was here.

"Speak freely."

"Have you heard anything more from Vern Eisenberger?"

"He's just put out is all." John breathed in audibly. "I daresay Vern's more upset over a farmer changing brands of feed than anything." He shook his head. "The man's carryin' a chip on his shoulder . . . spouting off 'bout us Amish in general to his English customers."

Philip wondered if Vern had seen the newspaper account of the runaway horse a while back. Everyone else in the area had read the story, or so it seemed. For weeks after the incident, even strangers had come up to him, stopping to ask questions at the hardware store and the like, wanting to know if he was in fact the Philip Bradley who'd lost control of Ezra Lapp's driving horse.

Maybe *that* was part of Eisenberger's beef, come to think of it. A name like Bradley stuck out like a sore thumb around here. His name was anything but Plain in conservative circles where Beiler, Lapp, and Zook were the most common surnames. He hadn't thought of it as posing trouble before. Rachel had cheerfully taken his name when they married, never once citing it as potential for trouble. Their baby son, Gabriel Bradley, would grow up in the close-knit society, most likely court and marry a Plain girl—give *her* the modern name. So it would go, from one generation to the next.

"I wish I'd never seen that pickup," he said sorrowfully.

John cuffed him firmly on the shoulder. "Put this Eisenberger incident to rest. Forgiving yourself is mighty important. Laughin' at shortcomings is, too. A gut belly laugh now and then makes a body live longer."

Philip was all for that. "But how can I make amends with Vern?"

"Ask almighty God 'bout that." Straightening, John walked to the door of the shed and peered out. "The Good Book says in Matthew, 'Let your light so shine before men, that they may see your good works, and glorify your Father which is in heaven.' Ain't so?"

Nodding in agreement, he followed John out of the shed and into the sunlight.

Before daybreak they came. On foot, by horse-drawn buggy, and some on horseback. Word had spread through the churches last Sunday, in each of the local districts. Seventy-five men came with their own tools and work aprons tied around their middles, some hauling in planks, posts, and hickory pegs to raise Zook's barn. Women and children came, too, in wagons loaded down with food hampers, hot coffee, and iced tea.

"Obadiah is never sure just how many workers will turn up on a day like this," John told Philip. "He leaves that to God . . . and the weather, too."

Philip was astounded at the number of women and young children scattered out over the area. Somewhere in the multitude of spectators and workers, his Rachel sat nursing their son, Gabriel. Annie, no doubt, was already playing with her first cousins and school friends. Christ's feeding of the five thousand came to mind as dawn broke in a blaze of golden sunshine.

Zook's teenage sons kept themselves busy directing buggy traffic, tying up and watering horses along the treed area of the lane, welcoming friends, relatives, and English farmers who'd received word of the barn raising. A bus drove up and stopped at the end of the lane, depositing Amishmen from the neighboring church districts of Hickory Hollow and SummerHill. The men wore black trousers and long-sleeved white shirts—some sleeves already rolled up—tan suspenders, and straw hats. Each was prepared for a long day of hard manual labor.

Days before, skilled men had finished repairing the old foundation. Beams and posts were cut ahead of time, as well, completing the bulk of the task before the frolic ever began.

In systematic fashion, much of the lumber was stacked in piles, marked in accordance to the order of use. All that remained was putting the pieces together to build a new barn—and a lot of brawn and hard work. Every aspect of the work would be done manually with only the aid of air-powered tools such as saws and drills. A diesel-powered air compressor provided the energy for the necessary equipment.

Out in the pasture, elderly folk began setting up folding chairs in rows, like spectators at a sporting event. There were cars lining the street, too, curiosity seekers watching from the road, photographers with cameras poised. Raising a big barn in a single day was nothing to sneeze at.

Amish children played games of checkers on blankets, while others pulled little brothers or sisters in wagons around the yard, stopping occasionally to get a cold drink at the old well pump. There was the steady drone of Pennsylvania Dutch, some farmers meeting with others for the first time in months or even years, depending on who had shown up for the last barn frolic.

Obadiah's assistant wasted little time dividing the men into groups, assigning specific jobs to each. Philip was teamed up with five other men who were responsible for preparing planks and panels that would ultimately create the frame of the barn. Moses Raber was the older man assigned to oversee Philip.

They set right to work. Now and then, Philip attempted to make eye contact with the carpenter who had spoken out so harshly against him. But to no avail. Obviously, Moses was still offended. Along with being burly—in excellent shape—the fifty-some-year-old carpenter towered over Philip and the others in the group. His face, seamed with lines, was pale in comparison to the ruddy-faced farmers, and heavy calluses and cuts were evident on the man's severely gnarled hands. Each of his finger joints were swollen, as well. *Moses has crippling arthritis*, Philip thought, never having noticed before today.

On a number of occasions, he offered to help carry a plank to ease the weight on Moses' hands. The gruff man, however, refused any such assistance, muttering in Dutch under his breath.

Why *had* Obadiah and his assistant put the two of them together on the same work team? It seemed strange. Yet Philip was determined to break through the barrier. Somehow he would not let this apparent rift continue. He would show Moses with compassion that he was, in fact, one of the brethren.

By seven o'clock, as streams of sunlight trickled across hill and dale, dozens of men utilized ropes and poles to hoist and heave the first frame into position. Consisting of tall posts joined to a crossbeam, the single framework extended the full length of the structure—sixty by ninety feet. Nimble-footed workmen climbed the frame, their bodies draped precariously over giant girders like so many grasshoppers. Carefully, they fitted each section of the growing frame, piece by piece.

By nine-thirty the men stopped work for a snack. Philip stood in line at the pump to wash his face and hands, while Moses headed in the opposite direction, head down, glancing back over his shoulder at Philip. Apparently, Moses was harboring a grudge, in spite of Rachel's declaration that "the People don't usually..."

Don't usually . . .

He wondered if Moses had succeeded in souring others in the community toward him. "Live the life before your brethren, come what may," Philip's pastor had advised. Philip intended to continue doing so, regardless of how many more mistakes he might make as a newcomer. Having felt somewhat of an oddity upon first settling here, he recalled his wife's kind and loving reassurance, along with that of her parents, Benjamin and Susanna Zook—Lavina Troyer, too. The People were discerning, he was told. They could detect both the spirit of a charlatan and a true-hearted soul. "You're ever so sincere," Rachel said on more than one occasion. "And if it weren't so, my mother would see right through you!"

They'd had a private laugh over it, but he believed Rachel was right. His mother-in-law could spot a phony a mile off.

Funny how some people were. Upon taking a job as a junior reporter at *Family Life Magazine*, fresh out of college, high-powered journalists and their personal copy editors had initially made him feel out of place. They hadn't meant to, of course. It was just this feeling of connectedness that a group acquires when they work together day in, day out. It tends to lead, sometimes innocently, sometimes not, to the clique mentality, to the schoolboy's "nanny, nanny, boo-boo . . . we were here *first*" mindset. Moses Raber reminded him clearly of those first few weeks at the Manhattan editorial offices so long ago.

He knew he didn't *have* to look for ways to get in the good graces of Moses Raber. What Philip felt now had nothing to do with the expectations of the People. His inner desire was to overlook the older man's intolerance—if that's what was actually bothering Moses—and move on.

"Faith looks up," he'd read somewhere recently. Sorrow

looks back to "what might've been," and worry looks around to gather more woe. But faith . . . faith sees prospects for the future and moves ahead.

◆

Philip and the others in the plank crew rested again briefly, well before the noon meal was scheduled, when they had gotten far enough ahead of the supply. During that time, Moses shuffled over to a tree in the side yard and sat alone.

Should I go to him now? Philip wondered, relying on God for wisdom. Not to be conspicuous, he stood around with the other men in his crew, glancing only occasionally at Moses.

High atop the lofty beams, the roof crew braced their bare feet against the widest joists, nailing the wall planks into place. Young boys combed the ground below for small items such as hammers and nails, scraps of boards, and occasionally a straw hat or two that the wind had lifted off someone's sweaty head.

Obadiah and his assistant kept the workmen on task, calling out instructions. Two older teenage boys, who were particularly deft on their feet, scrambled over boards, scaling the sides of planks, taking Obadiah's important commands to the men working high on the apex beams of the roof. The building of the new barn was well under way, running like clockwork.

Philip and Moses teamed up again after the short breather. Philip recalled his first roofing jobs after settling into the area. Those days and weeks had been very similar to *this* day as he had worked alongside an older, more experienced roofer, learning the skill without the benefit of hardly any verbal communication. He was slowly beginning to acclimate to the fact that most directions were conveyed in a nonverbal way in the Plain community. A rather silent persuasion, as Philip recalled.

For a man his age, Amishness began with an eagerness to accept responsibility, no matter the job complexity. A new convert's position in the community was based upon what he produced. Hard manual labor was a big part of being accepted into the fellowship of the brethren, and with a willingness to work hard came a strong sense of being needed, of dependence one upon another.

Working together with Moses Raber, so far, had been anything but a good experience. The carpenter spoke little and when he did, it was Dutch, which was to be expected, though Philip thought Moses *might* be more understanding, given Philip's status.

"If ya mean business, you'll learn the language," Moses said at one juncture. "If you're serious 'bout being Amish, that is."

"I'm completely serious," he insisted.

Moses stopped and pulled hard on his beard. "When you've practiced the language, we'll *all* know you're one of us," he said.

There was no mention of Vern Eisenberger and the "borrowed" pickup, but Philip got the message loud and clear.

At noon the men ceased their work entirely and sat on church benches at long tables, eating in shifts. Philip and his crew ate during the "second sitting." There was enough food for three hundred or more men and their families. Kettles of macaroni noodles continued to boil as the first few shifts of men ate meatloaf and noodles, cherry Jell-O, and date pudding. There were pies and a variety of additional desserts, as well.

Not until all the men were finished eating and back to work did the women and children ever sit down to the "set" menu. This was not an occasion for an assortment of potluck dishes. The menu was carefully planned, overseen by several women relatives and friends, each bringing specified items, such as countless bowls of date pudding or dozens of baking pans of meatloaf.

After the meal Moses went again to sit under the same shade tree, looking rather peaked, rubbing his face with his hands. Then he began to fan himself slowly with his straw hat.

Thinking this was the right time to make his move, Philip hurried past a bush where men's hats were still airing. He gazed down at the man enjoying a bit of protection from the sun under the tree. "Excuse me, Moses. May I have a word with you?"

"Talk is cheap" came the terse reply.

Philip squatted at eye level with the man. "I think I understand why you're put out with me."

"Well, now, is that so?"

He paused, making no progress at all with the ill-mannered man. "You know, I got behind the wheel of the feed salesman's pickup for only one reason," he said. "I wanted to help save Zook's barn."

"Shoulda thought more 'n twice 'bout something that serious." Moses snapped off a long, fat blade of grass and stared blankly at it. "Ain't never a bad thing to ponder something before doin' it. Anybody oughta know that."

Anybody . . .

There was no budging the man toward civility. Philip could see that. Yet he made a final attempt. "Some may think I'm here for only a short time. But the truth is—by the help of God—when I'm your age and older, I will be serving the Lord and my fellow man as a believer, right here in Bird-in-Hand."

"Say whatcha want," Moses shot back.

"I'm saying what I *believe*. The Lord has saved me from the beggarly elements of this world, as stated in the book of Galatians. I have turned my back on that miserable life to become a follower of Jesus Christ." He paused, noting that the singular blade of grass had slid out of Moses' crippled fingers and onto his trouser leg.

Inadvertently, Philip had turned on the heat with his pronouncement, but whatever he'd said seemed to register with Moses. The man rose to his feet with a grunt and nodded his head. He didn't suddenly welcome Philip into the fellowship of believers, nothing like that, but Moses *did* mumble a half-hearted assent. "Well, now, if you're sincere—one of us—you'll learn to speak our language."

There it was again, the insistence that Philip learn to speak Dutch. "I do *understand* it well," he said. This due to the fact that Rachel and Annie spoke it "a mile a minute" around the house.

"*Awwer Kannscht du Deitsch schwetze*—but can you *speak* Dutch?" Moses asked bluntly. "Ain't never heard ya much."

"*En Bissel*—a little," he replied in earnest. He had thought of asking Rachel to give him a crash course in Pennsylvania Dutch many times. He would see to it promptly, if that's what would convince Moses and who knows how many others. "I'll be speaking Dutch come Christmas."

Moses put his hat on his head, a hint of a smile on his creased face. When it was time to return to the work crew, Philip walked side by side with Moses as they approached the barnyard.

It was late into the afternoon, and several boys carried buckets of drinking water to the workers. Philip was glad for a refreshing cold drink. The day had turned unseasonably warm; quite a surprise for this late in autumn. They'd worked up a sweat and needed water to "wet their whistle," as well as to replenish their bodies in order to finish the job.

While Moses drank from the ladle, it began to slip out of his crippled hand. Philip caught it in the nick of time and assisted, holding the ladle steady for his team member.

A cup of cold water in my name . . . The Scripture ran through his mind.

The two men's eyes met and held momentarily. There was no exchange of words, but Philip sensed that common ground had been established between himself and the outspoken man.

The barn was up before nightfall. Neighbors, spectators, and the workers themselves—along with their families—began to head for home. They left as they came, some in awe that Amish and English alike could work together in such harmony. An extraordinary day and experience for all concerned.

Philip gathered up his own tools and went to find Rachel, Annie, and Gabe.

Meanwhile, John Zook and his wife, Rebecca, stood beside the new barn and prayed a blessing over it, gathering their sons and daughters and Grandfather Zook near. "We have much to be thankful for," John said, head bowed. "God has blessed us with kind, helpful neighbors and friends. Let us thank the Lord always for this provision of His mercy."

"So be it," Grandfather Zook said.

"Amen," said John Zook.

Once home, Philip shared his experiences at the frolic with Rachel as she set out cold cuts for their supper.

She nodded. "Working together like that all day will bring out either the best or the worst in two people."

"That's the truth." He filled her in on some of the "best" parts.

"We work for a higher cause, ya know." Rachel's eyes shone.

He caught her from behind and turned her around, pulling her gently to him. "Will you teach me to speak your language?" he whispered.

She grinned. "And will my husband be wantin' to learn to drive a horse and buggy, too?"

A week later, on his walk to work at Lavina's brother's farm, Philip noticed a vehicle parked along the side of the road with its hood up. Three men, none of them Amish, were bent over, their noses nearly touching the engine.

"Need some help?" he called to them.

It was Vern Eisenberger who turned around. Surprised, Philip saw that the broken-down truck was the blue pickup. "Well, if it isn't the not-so-Amish guy," Vern jeered, turning to his friends.

Philip chuckled under his breath. *Let your light so shine before men . . .* "What's the problem?" he asked, going to look under the hood with the rest of them.

"Can't seem to tell," said one.

Vern spoke up. "Could be the fan belt."

Obviously, Vern was hesitant to admit not knowing much about mechanics. Philip detected as much. "Mind if I take a look?"

Vern gave a disbelieving grunt, glancing sideways at his fellow companions.

In short order, Philip determined the problem and made some adjustments, offering a brief explanation to quell the raised eyebrows of the men when the pickup roared to life. "I used to do a lot of driving—worked on my own cars, too, when I was living in the Big Apple—before I turned Plain. I was far from the fold of God," he told them.

"Well, that makes sense about you driving before and yet it doesn't," Vern said with a skeptical grin, surveying Philip's attire. "*You* were a . . . a non-Amish once?" He didn't believe a word of it.

"I was a journalist . . . worked in a Manhattan skyscraper."

Philip wasn't proud of it, only wanted to clarify.

To this, Vern laughed out loud, closing the hood of his pickup with a resounding thud. "I suppose you've got a bridge to sell in London, too?"

"You know, I never apologized for borrowing your truck, did I?"

Vern shook his head. "For an Amishman, that's not too common."

"Now is as good a time as any." Philip made a sincere apology, adding, "I was wrong. Will you forgive me?"

Vern's face reddened. "Aw, who knows, I might've done the same thing, given the circumstances."

Philip turned to go. "Have a good day . . . you and your friends."

"Now, wait just a minute," Vern called after him. "Just how much sway do you have over John Zook, do you think?"

Philip was puzzled. "What do you mean?"

"Seems to me Zook could do some hard thinking before changing his brand of feed."

"You'll have to take that up with him."

"I think I'll just go over there and make him a good offer. What do you think of that?" Vern extended his hand and Philip shook it. "Thank you, uh, Mr.—"

"Call me Philip."

"Okay, big-city man." Vern was grinning as he got into his blue pickup and drove away.

Philip was glad to be on foot, without the headaches of car repair. He was also grateful for the tranquillity of the open road and the opportunity to practice his Dutch, his city days long gone. Offering a prayer of blessing for the day, he headed down the road, under the covering of heaven.

Tea for Three

How precious little deeds of love and sympathy are.
How strong to bless, how easy to perform, how comfortable to recall.

—Louisa May Alcott

Ach, it's always the same story. Whenever I ask Mam for one of her mouth-watering recipes (those not found in any recipe book), she starts reciting a long list of ingredients, sprinkling her comments with—"mix in a handful of chopped onion, depending on its size, and stir in generous pinches of dried celery leaves," or "use a blob of mayonnaise the size of an egg."

But I'll stop her, now and then, tryin' my best to jot things down quickly so I can remember for always.

"*Nee*—no, no, Rachel,"—Mam's eyes are shining—"ya mustn't pay such close attention to the recipe . . . to the *words*."

"How else—?"

"Cooking and baking depends on so many things, such as how warm or cool your kitchen is," she continued. "And what quality are the ingredients? And the mindset of the cook and suchlike, ya know."

I'm fully aware of all this, having observed the creative process of food preparation hundreds of times while growin' up in an Old Order household, soaking up kitchen activities like a sponge soaks up spilt milk. Still, the idea of passing on the delicacies of such things as *Lattwarick* (apple butter), *Siesse-raahmkuche* (sweet cream cake), and other centuries-old treats seems awful important to me these days.

Now that I'm well on my way to havin' a houseful of children—two so far, and another on the way—along with cooking for Philip, whose appetite is hearty after a long day of workin' the land and other odd jobs, I'm kept ever so busy in the kitchen. Sometimes, too, Lavina Troyer, as well as Adele Herr, who lives with Lavina over in the Dawdi Haus, will join us for the evening meal. To hear the two women talk, you'd think they were privy to my concern 'bout writing down the People's recipes. Truly, Lavina will say clear out of the blue, in her faltering way, "Passin' down our recipes is somethin' akin to the Ordnung, really," which is the unwritten blueprint for expected Amish behavior. "Ain't written down anywheres . . . the People just know it, is all," Lavina says, her thin face all aglow.

'Course, she's right. And there are plenty other things that don't get recorded formally for posterity, yet they're handed down from one generation to the next. But in an unspoken manner. Take quilting. I might give my daughter, Annie, some pieces to make a quilt, along with one of her girl cousins, and, lo and behold, if Annie doesn't make a "nine-patch" and her cousin a "diamond in the square." The same pieces turn out two patterns, diff'rent as can be.

Nobody round here jots down the art of quilting to pass on

to their daughters and granddaughters. Not plowing and plant-
ing, neither. Plain young people just *know* by listenin', by
watching what their parents do. It's an "understanding," I
heard one minister put it. Almost ingrained.

The People hand down the tunes to the hymns, sung in
unison and by rote, from the Ausbund. No musical notation is
found in the Amish hymnbook, only the words. And we teach
our young men how to build a barn in one day, where mostly
nonverbal communication happens. Know-how is passed along
by skilled older men to the younger by the act of observance,
which my Philip learned at a recent barn frolic.

Getting back to the issue of wonderful-gut recipes bein'
lost to the next generation, I had a rare opportunity the other
day to slip away from the house early in the afternoon. Lavina
didn't mind watching over sleeping baby Gabe, and Annie was
still at school. So while I was free—just a bit—I headed on
over to visit Mam at Orchard House B&B, where Philip first
rented a room. He had been a journalist assigned to do re-
search on a story 'bout Amish Christmas celebrations back
then.

I went for the sole purpose of askin' Mam to recite her
meatball chowder recipe and, if she had the time, some others,
too. Anyways, I wasn't in the door more'n half a minute and
she slipped her arm through mine, leading me out to the
kitchen, where she insisted we have ourselves a cup of sweet
chamomile tea and some of her sand tarts, light and thin, still
warm from the oven.

I was more than happy to sit and sip tea with Mam.
Though she and Dat lived less than two miles from Philip and
me, Mam didn't have many opportunities to get away. They

ran a bustling bed-and-breakfast business, 'specially booked up with overnight guests during peak foliage. Right now. By the looks of the dark circles under her usually bright eyes, Mam was long overdue for a quiet moment or two.

"What wouldja think of me copying down some of your recipes?" I asked, settling into her sunny kitchen.

"Well, now, Philip isn't thinkin' of putting them in his collection of stories, is he?"

I bit my tongue. Where on earth had she gotten such a notion? "Mam—"

"I won't have a thing to do with folk getting rich off my recipes. They've been in the family as long as your great-great-grandmammi's arrival from Switzerland."

"But, Mam, the recipes aren't for Philip," I assured her. "*I* want them. And someday Annie will, too, when she grows up and bakes for *her* family."

Susanna crossed her arms and leaned against the counter, just a-starin' at me. "Honestly, Rachel?"

She knew I wouldn't lie. "I don't want your recipes to . . ." I thought better than to say *die off with you, Mam*—but that's what I was thinkin'. "It'd be a terrible thing for them to get lost over the years, ya know."

Mamma's eyelids fluttered a bit as she stood there, prob'ly thinking over my request. Then, without saying more, she came and sat at the table across from me, her eyes still wide with a trace of doubt.

"It's all right," I said. "I'll keep them in the family."

"Philip won't up and publish an Amish cookbook, then get yourself rich as can be?"

"No, Mamma . . . this is just for me." I wondered why she

was worried 'bout Philip makin' extra money in the first place. The thought was obviously stuck in her mind. Fact was, my husband's article and story writing didn't bring in the kind of income he was used to making while writing for the New York magazine. No, he'd given up a life of riches to marry me and join church here.

I kept lookin' at Mam, wondering just what it was that seemed to eat away at her just now. Were she and Dat struggling over finances? Hardly. I knew precisely what they asked, and got, for a room with a private bath per night. Goodness knows, there were always tourists eager to stay in an "authentic" Amish B&B. For a gut seven months out of the year, they were booked solid. No, that couldn't be what was botherin' her.

"More tea?" she asked, getting up before I ever said.

"Jah, little."

"Didja bring along pen and paper, then?" Mam seemed to ask her question to the wall right there by the kitchen sink. And she didn't wait for me to respond, neither. "Benjamin's thinking 'bout sellin' the business," she said, her voice flat as could be.

"The inn, ya mean?"

She nodded her head slowly. "This here house and everything."

"Is . . . is Dat awful sick?" A knot began to grow in my stomach.

"Just wore out, I 'spect, though it ain't him doin' most the work here."

I could see that Mam was more than a little put out with Dat just by the firm set of her jowl. The stubborn look in her eyes, too, reminded me of a day, years before, when I'd told her Jacob Yoder and I were plannin' to be married. Jacob, at that time, was walkin' the fence 'tween the Old Order and the Amish-Mennonites. He had been killed in a buggy wreck, along with our young son, one sad summer day a few years ago.

It was mighty clear Mam wasn't happy 'bout selling out and retiring. Just as she wasn't happy 'bout me marryin' outside our church district, and she tried to put a stop to it, which hadn't set well with Jacob. She was a strong and outspoken woman, not nearly as submissive as many of the womenfolk in the community were known to be.

"When's Dat thinking of sellin' the inn?" I asked at last.

"Soon as he can get a real estate agent over here to measure the place and run a market analysis, I s'pose."

I sighed. Wasn't it just yesterday they'd packed up and left the family farm, my childhood home, turnin' over the duties to my brother and his wife? They'd moved into this rambling two-story house, hangin' out the Orchard Guest House sign to draw attention to the inn.

"Where will you live?" I asked.

"Our own Dawdi Haus, if your father has his way."

Back to the farm, I thought.

"Are ya sure Dat's ready?"

Mam frowned. "I wouldn't be tellin' ya if he wasn't. Believe me, I've shed plenty a tear . . . prayed, too."

I was glad to hear the latter. "Prayer helps, Mamma. Keep talkin' to the Lord 'bout your fears."

"Who said a thing 'bout fears?" She came and poured more tea for me, spilling some over the sides, making a tiny pool around the base of the saucer.

I knew I should've kept my comments to myself. It was painful seein' Mam hurting so. "Maybe it's the end of the season that makes Dat feel this way," I spoke up. "Winter will be closin' in here perty soon. Could that be what he's thinkin'?"

"Winter and old age, to put it bluntly." Mam carried the teakettle back and placed it firmly on the stovetop. "Your father's much older than I am . . . 'least inside he is. If ya know what I mean."

"Jah." I'd sensed it happening all the while Annie and I lived with them, after Jacob and young Aaron were killed in the accident. Something had died within Benjamin Zook the day his bright-eyed grandson was buried six feet under. Just as part of me had ended, too.

"Dat's not still mourning, is he?" I found myself asking.

"Ach, not so much, really." She went to the window and looked out. "Truth be known, I think he's tired of living. Guess we all come to that, sometime or other."

"You'll go along with his idea, then?" I asked.

She turned and smiled. "You know me well, Rachel. And I must tell ya"—and here she leaned against the windowsill—"I've given up fussing over things so. Life's too short to insist on havin' your own way. Makes for trouble on ev'ry hand."

My guess was that her coming to the Lord, as she had some time ago, had changed her from the inside out. She'd yielded to the longing in her heart for a relationship with almighty God. Jah, Mam was much softer round the edges, in a manner of speaking. Most of the time, she was.

"I'll be in prayer for you . . . 'bout this," I said softly.

Eyes glistening now, she nodded her head, unable to speak.

"God knows where your future—and Dat's—is to be."

She pulled out a kitchen chair and sat next to me this time. We smiled silently at each other, her lower lip quivering as she reached for her teacup.

I took one more sand tart, marveling at its delicate thinness. Never had *mine* come out so perfectly. "I must have *this* recipe, too." I went on to say that I'd been making sand tarts for years but failed in comparison to her special touch.

Quietly, she began to list the ingredients—sayin' what she did and how she did it—all of that. And not once did she complain or stop me from takin' notes. Not this time. Pen in hand, I scribbled across the paper, like a chicken scratching the gut, clean earth. I was ever so glad for this visit. Mam's willingness to share . . . her openness. We'd come such a long way, the two us, together *and* independently. I could only hope and pray that Annie and I might have such a straightforward mother-daughter relationship when she was all grown-up and married.

Jah, this was the way I'd always wished it might be, sittin' here with the sun's rays circling round us, and crisp burnt-orange leaves fallin' silently off the trees, one family recipe after another spilling off Mam's lips.

Then, when it was clear that she was too tired to go on, I went lookin' for Dat.

I found him in the parlor, shades drawn low. "Wouldja care for an afternoon treat?" I asked.

His eyes smiled up at me. With a grunt, he got out of his chair and came with me, joining us in the cheerful kitchen. There, I offered him some of Mam's wonderful-gut sand tarts and poured him a cup of honey-sweetened tea.

PART III

Grasshopper Level

Acres of rich farmland spilled down toward the
valley, a panorama of beauty far as the eye could see.
Oak trees sang the colors of gold and bronze. Sugar
maples wore flaming crimson, their portly arms
extended out over the lane. . . .

—from *The Redemption of Sarah Cain*

The Courtship of Lyddie Cottrell

I am my beloved's, and my beloved is mine. . . .
—*Song of Solomon 6:3*

Lydia dearly loved Levi King. The sun rose and set on her love for him. But there had been days here lately when Lyddie honestly wondered if she was the right choice for Levi. And, too, her younger brothers and sisters—Caleb, Anna Mae, Josiah, and Hannah—were still just getting used to Aunt Sarah moving in, becomin' their new mamma. Not to mention Uncle Bryan becoming their father figure almost overnight, him having married Mamma's deceased fancy "English" sister—Sarah Cain—just last May.

What *would* happen if she wed Levi next month, leaving behind the siblings she'd so cared for and loved since Mamma's heavenly home going? *Will they feel abandoned?* she sometimes wondered. She lay awake nights long after Aunt Sarah and Uncle Bryan had turned off the lights and taken themselves off to bed. Sometimes she stared at the window in the far wall of her own bedroom, just a-pondering her siblings' future. Truth be known, brooding 'bout her own future, too.

185

In the past month or so, her seven-year-old sister Hannah had become mighty insecure. Clingy, really. And it wasn't that Hannah hadn't taken to Aunt Sarah; Lydia didn't think *that* was the problem at all. Hannah's insecurity had more to do with all the talk of Lyddie's marriage to Levi.

Just last week, Lyddie and Aunt Sarah had been drying dishes together, casually discussin' the wedding dinner menu, when—unknown to either of them—Hannah was standing in the doorway, listening.

Lyddie spotted her youngest sister there, seeing her lower lip protruding sadly. "Well, what's this?" she asked, going to Hannah and squatting down next to her.

Hannah said nothing but buried her head in Lyddie's shoulder, holdin' on to her ever so tight. And later that night, Hannah had insisted that Lyddie tuck her into bed, whispering that she didn't want Lyddie to go off and marry "that Levi King."

"You'll be just fine here with Aunt Sarah and Uncle Bryan. They love you much." She'd tried to soothe Hannah's fears as she plumped the small pillow, Hannah's arms limp as can be outside the sheet. "Caleb, Josiah, and Anna Mae will be here with you, too, don't forget."

Still, no matter what Lyddie said or did to try 'n' calm her sister, the little girl was sad. And the sadder Hannah became, the harder it was for Lyddie to enjoy her courtin' days. Truth be told, not only did Hannah have worries 'bout Lyddie's upcoming marriage, Lyddie herself was nursing a few fears of her own.

When she talked things over with her dear friend, Fannie didn't seem to understand at all. "Sounds like you've got cold feet," Fannie said. And this after Lyddie had gone so far as to reveal her most personal fears, at a time when she'd felt she *had* to confide or burst, one or the other.

They'd gone for a walk, takin' in the spicy autumn bouquet that rose up out of the soil and into the air all round them. Grasshopper Level—the area where Lyddie's parents' family home was located—had a special glow 'bout it this time of year. She'd first noticed it when she was much younger. Ten or eleven, maybe. Back when Mamma was alive and healthy, enjoying a mornin' walk with the children down to the one-room school. Peach Lane School, 'twas called. The very schoolhouse where Lyddie was now a teacher.

'Course, all that was 'bout to change, since the People didn't allow young women to continue on as teachers once they were married. The idea bein', the bride must set her sights on husband, housework, and bearing children soon as possible.

"Am I the only bride-to-be who has wondering—fears, I 'spect you could say?" she asked Fannie.

"I wouldn't know firsthand, but from what I've heard from my older sisters, there *are* times when a person questions a decision to marry, no matter how long ago 'twas made."

Lyddie thought on that. She'd promised to marry handsome and thoughtful Levi King back last February. Promised never to hurt him again, which, sadly, she had done before. "Levi has no idea what I'm tellin' you," she admitted.

Fannie, tall and thin, glanced sideways at her. "Fears or no, Levi's the boy for you. First time I heard you two were goin' home from Singing together, I was sure you and Levi would end up together, prob'ly. He's as gut as gold. The bishop thinks so, too."

Gut as gold . . .

Jah, she'd heard the same thing said 'bout her beloved. "I just wish I could share with him the way I do with you."

Fannie sighed so loud Lyddie wondered what that was all 'bout. "If I were you, I wouldn't worry 'bout talkin' out everything on your heart just now. Save some of it for *after* you're married."

They stopped walking, standing in full sun now, enjoying the warmth of it. For a moment, Lyddie wished she were barefooted. Looking past Fannie to the rolling hills below them, she said, "I think of Mamma so often, ya know. Prob'ly too much these days. When Dat died, I think something tore loose inside Mamma. Her heart must've stopped workin' that very day. Took several years for it to catch up with her . . . killing her in the end."

"Aw, Lyddie, for goodness' sake. Why do ya talk so?"

"I was the one who saw how Mamma suffered when Dat went on to Glory. Nobody knows . . ."

"What's that got to do with you marryin' or not marryin' Levi?" Fannie stared hard at her.

"What if *I* have a bad heart like Mamma's and don't know till it's too late?" Lydia paused, realizing she'd revealed the deepest fear of her heart, here on the open road, under the blue arch of sky.

"I don't put two and two together and get four," Fannie retorted. "I still don't see what you're so worried 'bout."

"Mamma died at a young age . . . maybe *I* will, too. That would break Levi's heart and our children's, too, just the way it's hurt my brothers and sisters . . . and me."

"You're not thinkin' clearly today," Fannie said.

"Maybe not." Lyddie was hurt. Her friend didn't understand one iota.

They walked down the road in utter silence, back toward her farmhouse, where Fannie's parents' carriage was parked in the side yard, the mare waiting in the barn.

Should've kept my fears to myself, Lyddie thought. Yet she knew Fannie to be trustworthy. Jah, it was all right that she poured out her woes—real or otherwise—to her friend.

"I'll be in prayer for ya, Lyddie," Fannie said when they arrived at the end of the lane.

"Denki, I'm glad for that." The girls embraced quickly, then Fannie headed up to the barn to get the horse.

Lyddie stood beside the buggy, waiting to help Fannie hitch up. While she did, she noticed Aunt Sarah peeking out through the window, prob'ly wondering why the girls had needed to be gone so long. Fact was, Lyddie needed to bare her soul. She just couldn't get the memory of Mamma's death out of her mind. How would *Levi* feel if he lost *her* to heart failure? How would he feel if she didn't tell him such a disease might run in the family? It almost seemed better for Levi never to marry her, whom he loved so awful much, than to lose his wife to premature death. The more she thought on it, the more she wondered if Levi himself had considered any of this. Yet her beloved had never voiced anything such as this on their rides in his courting buggy. Never once.

"Oh, what's-a-matter with me?" she whispered, watching Fannie lead the horse down through the barnyard toward the buggy. "Why must I worry so?"

"Is something troubling you, Lyddie?" Aunt Sarah asked the next day before any of the children or Uncle Bryan had come downstairs for breakfast.

The sun was already squeezing its bright yellow head through the grove of trees out to the east, sending gleaming rays across the big yard and down toward the springhouse.

Standing in the front window, Lyddie gazed hard at the landscape. "Soon we'll be unpacking the comforters and quilts for the winter, won't we?" she said.

Aunt Sarah was still, saying not a word. Lyddie was glad for that. Not much of what was comin' out of her own mouth these days made much sense. What *did* comforters and quilts— getting them out of attic trunks—have to do with her mood? Truth was, she was starting to feel the pressure of time hard upon her. Her and Levi's wedding day was fast approaching, just weeks from now.

"I'm befuddled," she confessed. "Mamma would say I have the jitters, is all. But . . . I think it may be more than that."

Aunt Sarah moved to stand next to her in the window. "It's hard to know what someone else might say to you. But I remember clearly how difficult it was for me to say yes to marriage."

Surprised, Lyddie turned to look into her aunt's face. "Really, 'twas?"

"No one knows how I struggled." Her aunt paused, putting her arm around Lyddie's shoulder. "I knew in my heart Bryan was the man for me, but I fought it for many years."

She wouldn't ask her aunt—wasn't any of Lyddie's business, really—what the struggle was. Didn't need to. The look of empathy on Sarah's perty face was enough. The two women shared a common bond.

Aunt Sarah asked, "When you think of Levi, do you ever consider what your life would be without him . . . or his without you? If you weren't being courted, planning to be Levi's wife, how would you feel right now?"

"I think that way sometimes." Lydia wouldn't go on to say what her reasoning was for doing so.

How Aunt Sarah knew anything of the battle goin' on inside her, Lyddie did not know. Her mamma's fancy sister, all dolled up in makeup and curled hair, wearing English clothes . . . well, Sarah had somehow seen right through to Lyddie's wavering.

"You know I'm here to help," Aunt Sarah said before the two of them shuffled into the kitchen and started cookin' breakfast.

A better mother substitute Lyddie could not imagine. It was somehow uncanny, really, this connection she shared with her mother's sister, an outsider who showed no interest in joining church or livin' the Plain life. She and Bryan conducted their lives like fancy folk. Aunt Sarah worked as a real estate agent during the day, and Uncle Bryan was a computer systems analyst, sometimes traveling, sometimes not. They saw to it that Lyddie and her siblings attended the New Order Amish church. But after dropping them off at the meetinghouse, Uncle Bryan and Aunt Sarah headed over to a community church near Strasburg, where they worshiped, then returned in time to pick Lyddie and the children up for Sunday dinner. So far the system was working out all right, though Lyddie felt peculiar riding in a car on the Lord's Day. Still, there wasn't much she or her brothers and sisters could do. Sometimes things just had to be the way they were. Mamma wouldn't have minded all that much. A practical sort of woman, Mamma put her children first, right after God, but up there with the bishop's rulings and the preacher's admonishments. One of the reasons why Aunt Sarah was their stepmother now was because Mamma knew her sister would love and care for her nieces and nephews with all diligence.

"Let me know if you want to talk again," Aunt Sarah said in the kitchen, amid waffle making and egg frying.

"I wish Levi and I could talk things over," she replied.

"Well, why not?"

She didn't tell Aunt Sarah what Fannie had said. That it was best *not* to share so deeply with a beau before the wedding. Besides, Levi would be coming over this Sunday night, after supper. She would ask the Lord to guide her long before then.

Last Sunday evening they'd sat on the couch side by side, taking turns reading to each other. Lyddie 'specially liked the book of Psalms, and she'd put extra expression into her voice. " 'Great is the Lord, and greatly to be praised in the city of our God, in the mountain of his holiness. Beautiful for situation, the joy of the whole earth, is mount Zion, on the sides of the north, the city of the great King.' "

"Sounds like poetry," Levi had said. "You make the reading sound so . . . well, so perty." With this compliment, Levi's face, not Lyddie's, blushed several shades of red.

"Denki." She was glad she could please him this way. "Wouldja care to hear another?"

He had nodded and smiled, his eyes all a-twinkle with love for her.

After the evening meal the following Sunday, Levi arrived with his shiny black courting buggy and his fastest steed. "Someone's here to see our Lyddie," Caleb, her fourteen-year-old brother, said, peering out the window.

Our Lyddie . . .

She folded her shawl over her arm, standing in the front room, waiting there with Aunt Sarah. "Pray for me while I'm gone," she whispered to her aunt.

"Let me give you some advice," Aunt Sarah said. "Talk tonight . . . don't kiss so much."

"Aw, now!" Lyddie looked up into her aunt's face and had to chuckle. How *did* she know such things?

"Don't be afraid to share your thoughts." Aunt Sarah's words were good and right. Lyddie knew they were.

"You're sayin' to me what Mamma would've, prob'ly." And with that, she reached up to Aunt Sarah and planted a little kiss on her soft cheek.

"Have a good time, Lyddie."

"Denki . . . I will." With that, she heard Levi knocking at the back door, saw Caleb and Josiah scurrying out of the kitchen and up the stairs.

"Boys!" Uncle Bryan called to them, fast on their heels.

She had to smile, making her way into the suddenly deserted kitchen. Such a family she had. Ach, how she loved them, each one.

Opening the door, she saw Levi standing before her, looking ever so striking in his Sunday-go-to-meetin' trousers, long-

sleeved shirt, and suspenders. He hadn't worn his hat this evening, and she could see how shimmering clean his cropped
hair was, his ears poking out from under the layer. "Hullo, Lyddie."

"Levi . . . gut to see ya." She went to his outstretched arms.

"Ready, then?" he asked, smiling down at her.

"Jah."

The evening was turning a bit chilly as he helped her into
the left side of the open carriage. "Didja bring along a sweater
or—"

"My shawl." Lyddie held it up a bit, speaking out of turn.
Thinking that she ought to have waited for Levi to finish, she
felt a twinge of guilt. Mamma had taught, by her own example,
to be slow to speak, offering patience, humility, and submission
when it came to the most important man in her life. Dat was
certainly a godly man, and Mamma's respect and compliance
came easily.

Levi was also a devout young man, his mind set on spiritual goals. Most of the time, at least. She also knew that she
was a distraction, so fond he was of her.

The evening sky was full up with shades of color—ink
blue, hues of pink and yellow—as the horse pulled the carriage
down the lane and out onto the road. The sound of *clip-clopping* interrupted the quietude, but the rhythm of the horse's
hooves on the pavement made for a nice, comfortable backdrop.

They heard other sounds in the twilight—katydids, crickets, and whippoorwills. And some courting buggies were out
on the roads by now, but not many. Most couples would've
gone to one or more singings by this hour. After the singing in

the house and activities in the barn, they'd get back in their buggies and ride round with their beaus till the wee hours, makin' some of the girls' mammas fret.

"Wanna go for a long ride?" Levi asked.

Aunt Sarah had encouraged her to talk, so a long ride was a gut idea. "Jah, that's fine." The jitters returned at the thought of opening her heart wide to the handsome fella at her side.

"Down to Strasburg?" he asked.

"That's a long ways." She'd gone with Aunt Sarah in the car to Strasburg several times in the past month, but the ride by horse and carriage was at least an hour long.

Levi slipped one arm around her, holding the reins with the other. "We've got all night," he said.

She didn't argue with him. But they didn't have *all* night. Uncle Bryan was expecting her home before midnight. "*Well* before midnight," her uncle had said, and Lyddie quickly agreed.

Levi had plenty on his mind, but not much of it had to do with talking. "Come here closer to me, *lieb*—dear," he said. "I've missed ya so." This he whispered in her ear, sending shivers up and down her back.

Oh, how she wanted to snuggle with him, let him kiss her some, but too many loose ends dangled in her mind. And once he started with the smoochin', well, she knew how hard it would be to think anything but romantic thoughts.

"Levi . . . I . . ." She paused. "Wouldja mind too awful much if we talked a bit?" she asked him, sitting up straight.

"Well, sure, Lyddie."

She breathed deeply, staring at the line of maple trees silhouetting the sky up ahead. Could she speak the things on her heart? Dared she?

"Lyddie, dearest, what is it?" He'd turned to face her now, both arms drawing her near, the reins hanging unattended.

She knew if she relaxed in his arms, let his lips find hers, another courting night might pass, and the things she'd already discussed with both Fannie and Aunt Sarah would fall by the wayside. Important things. After all, their publishing Sunday, when church members and all the community would formally hear of their wedding plans, was fast approaching. She couldn't wait much longer to declare her fears to her beloved. She *must* not.

"Have you ever wondered what would happen if . . ." Her words sounded peculiar to her own ears, so she stopped.

"If *what* would happen?" he asked, ears tuned to her every breath.

"You remember when my father was killed in the farming accident?"

Levi nodded. "Jah. My uncle and cousin were the first to find him in the field."

"Didja ever think that my mamma might've died of a broken heart?" She sat back against the seat, somewhat spent at her own question.

"Wouldn't be surprised at that." His voice was a thin thread in the night. "Everyone knew how much your parents loved each other."

"Everyone?" She was surprised at his response.

"Jah, my mamma and aunts kept talking 'bout the 'great love' the Cottrells had for each other. And how awful sad it was." He took her hand and held it against his own heart.

"Your mother was ever so loyal to her first and only love. She never even thought of remarrying. . . ." He put her hand to his face and kissed it lightly. "That's the kind of love you and I will have after a gut many years together, Lyddie dear."

"Jah, I want that, too," she whispered, nearly choking on her words. "But what if Mamma *didn't* die of a broken heart . . . what if she had a bad heart because it runs in the family?"

"What're you sayin'?"

She swallowed hard, forcing back the lump in her throat. "Well, I . . . I would just hate to see you suffer and grieve so, if . . . if I was to die early, like Mamma."

He was silent for a time, then—"Lyddie, *none* of us knows what the morrow holds. For some folk, God sees fit to take them home long before the rest of us might think necessary. But our Lord's will is over and above all. We hafta trust in that."

She knew what he said was true. Made her wonder if he'd already pondered the issue. "I'd hate to cause you that sort of pain, if I left you a young widower . . . and our children without a mamma."

"You're thinkin' of your own siblings now, aren't you?"

"Jah." Mostly she was thinking of little Hannah.

"I'm glad you brought this up." He released her hand and cupped her chin in both his hands. "We'll lean hard on the Lord just as your parents did."

"I must submit my fears to the Lord."

"We'll cherish every minute we *do* have together, jah?" He kissed her then, a sweet kiss filled with promise. He might've agreed with her that, without a doubt, she was a worrywart. Instead, he talked of the many relatives and friends he planned to have help on their wedding day—parking buggies and watering and feeding the driving horses. His enthusiasm calmed her a bit, pulling her into lively conversation.

An hour or so later they had planned everything, from which preacher might lead the first phase of the worship service, to who would preach the main sermon, and which of Lyddie's mother's friends was to oversee the cooking for the day. A celebration meal, to be sure, consisting of roast duck and chicken, mashed potatoes, gravy, and dressing, coleslaw, cold ham, raw and cooked celery, prunes, pickles, peaches, bread and butter, jams, cherry pie, tea, cookies, and an abundance of cakes.

"Oh, Lyddie, just think what a day it'll be!" Levi turned to pick up the reins, clicking his tongue to get the mare trottin' a bit faster.

She leaned her head on her beloved's shoulder, just as excited, yet wondering how she could ever look into the eyes of her young siblings, 'specially Hannah's, leaving them totally in the care of their English aunt and uncle.

These things she would not delve into just now. Enough was enough for one night. She would enjoy the rest of the ride, hope that Levi might keep talking. "Wanna ride past ol' Mathias Byler's place?" he asked. "Hear his serenade?"

She said she'd like that. Mathias always sat out on his front porch, playin' his harmonica for the courting couples as they rode by.

"Won't be but a minute now, and we'll have us a perty tune," Levi said, grinning at her as the moon slipped across the sky.

"My uncle wants me to be home before midnight," she whispered.

He turned and puckered his lips comically. "You sure 'bout that?"

"Ever so sure."

"I'll see to it, then," he said more earnestly.

Soon they caught the sound of music floating out over the night to them from Mathias Byler's long porch. The tune was sweet, almost sad.

"Why do ya think he makes music, rain or shine?" she asked softly, wondering.

"He's lonely, prob'ly . . . likes to encourage courtin' couples to drive by," replied Levi.

"Lonely for his wife?" The pain touched her heart anew. "After all these years . . ."

They passed a courting buggy heading in the opposite direction. "Hullo, Levi and Lydia!" the driver called to them.

"Who's that?" she asked Levi.

"My cousin Joshua and his *Aldi*—girlfriend. They're getting published next Sunday."

"Where're they headed, do you think?"

"For some ice cream. Wanna turn round and join them?"

She shivered at the thought of ice cream. "Do you?"

"Why not?" It was clear Levi wanted to, so she nodded, almost relieved for this pleasant distraction, in spite of how cold the ice cream would be on an autumn evening. This way she wouldn't be tempted to bring up more concerns over leaving four siblings behind. Levi would be callin' her a worrier for sure, if she did.

Aunt Sarah wasn't at all pushy the following day. Never asked a single question 'bout Lyddie's evening with Levi. The two women were hanging out Monday's wash on the line before Lyddie had to hurry off to the Amish schoolhouse to start up the wood stove. As a good teacher, she wanted to take the chill off the room before the children arrived.

At school Hannah caused somewhat of a disturbance during morning lessons. Not that the little girl was disobedient. Wasn't that at all. Hannah, with long brown braids wrapped round her head, sniffled continuously, annoyingly so, as if she suffered a terrible head cold or had been crying. Lyddie guessed the latter. Hannah truly had not been herself for weeks now. But crying in school?

She motioned for Hannah to come to her desk. "Are you feelin' awful sad today?" she whispered.

Hannah nodded her head up and down. "Jah, ever so much."

Lyddie put her arm around her sister. Not only was Hannah going to miss her at home, but the wee one was losing her big sister as a teacher, too. "Didja finish your ABC's?" she asked gently.

"I wrote them nice and straight."

Lyddie had an idea. "When recess comes, why don't you stay inside and help me?"

The girl's face brightened at the suggestion. "Jah, I'll help you, Lyddie."

"Remember to call me 'Teacher' at school, all right?"

"Jah, Teacher," Hannah said, going back to her desk to sit down, a smile all over her face.

After lunch, when the last student left the schoolhouse to go outdoors, Lyddie scooted a chair up to her desk for her sister. "Just think, Hannah, you can come and visit your new brother, Levi, and me anytime . . . after we're married. Won't that be fun?"

Hannah's eyes got ever so wide just then. "Levi's gonna be *my* brother?"

"Jah." This was obviously something her sister hadn't thought of, that Levi King was to become a relative of *hers*. So Lyddie told Hannah what that would mean. "We'll be a bigger family, that's all. And we'll get together on Sundays for dinner and on holidays, too. You'll see." She paused. "I'll still help you with your readin' and writin', just not here at school."

"Oh." Hannah's mouth was still droopy.

"You won't be losin' me as your sister; you'll be getting another brother."

"Does Caleb know 'bout this?"

Lyddie had to laugh a little. "Both Caleb and Josiah are mighty glad to have a third boy join the Cottrell family." She went on to explain that the girls would be outnumbered by one.

"But maybe not for long," Hannah said. "If Uncle Bryan and Aunt Sarah have a baby girl someday, then we'll have *three* girls."

"That's right!" She gave Hannah a big hug.

When she looked up she saw Levi standing at the door of the schoolhouse. Reluctantly, she left Hannah, whose eyes weren't nearly so puffy and red now. "I'll be right back," she said, walking toward her darling.

Standing on the sagging white porch, she told Levi she daren't leave Hannah alone too long.

"Why . . . what's wrong?" he asked, concern written on his face.

She didn't want to open up the topic for discussion. Not here, not where she was in charge of a whole schoolyard full of youngsters, her own sister in most need of attention. "I'll tell you another time," she said, hoping not to sound curt.

"Hannah isn't sick, is she?"

"No . . . not sick."

"Then *what?*" Levi drew near, his eyes searching hers.

She glanced over her shoulder at her baby sister, now staring at both of them. "I think we best talk later."

Levi pressed on. "Is it . . . could it be botherin' Hannah that her big sister is getting married soon?"

Awfully discerning, he was. The realization startled Lyddie, and she lowered her voice to a whisper. "Hannah's been crying all mornin'."

Levi, still frowning, said he had something in the buggy for her. "It's from my mam. I'll go and get it. Won't take but a minute."

She watched as he darted through the yard toward the buggy, returning with a big basket filled with goodies. "Treats for you and the children," he said, handing over the basket.

"Mam knew you like popcorn balls, so she made enough for the whole school."

"Mmm, yum!" Lyddie said, motioning for Hannah to come have a look-see. "Levi's mamma made a surprise for us."

Hannah came shyly at first, then she peered inside the basket at all the wrapped, round goodies.

Levi grinned at both Lyddie and Hannah. Then, without warning, he stooped down and picked Hannah up. "Wanna play horsey?" He set her high on his shoulders and went galloping outside, through the schoolyard, beyond the swings and around the perimeter, past both the boys' outhouse and the girls'.

Hannah's squeals of delight sailed higher than even the sound of the older boys at play. Lyddie couldn't help herself; she was filled with amazement and joy.

Oh, she could just imagine her future with a loving husband like Levi. A wonderful-gut father to their children, too, someday. And from the look of glee on Hannah's face as she bounced up and down on Levi's strong shoulders, Lyddie's fears were completely unfounded. Her beloved was, just this minute, winning Hannah over, becoming a third big brother. Truly, he was.

At Twilight

The tumult of thy mighty harmonies
Will take from both a deep, autumnal tone,
Sweet though in sadness.

—Percy Bysshe Shelley

Mathias Byler has been playing his harmonica to serenade young Amish couples nigh unto twenty years now. The
lilting refrain of a mouth organ makes for a right nice backdrop for a young beau and his girl as they ride horse and buggy
up and down the road in front of his farmhouse. Mathias likes
to think his harmonica sounds like the cooing of sea birds
across a quiet bay in springtime. And that's just what he thinks
of as he eases his breath in and out, playing mostly hymns,
slow and sweet. Doesn't much matter to him what he plays,
really; it's more *what* he's providin' for the youngsters—a whole
parade of 'em tonight—that gives Mathias the necessary
breath to keep the music goin' for a gut hour or more of an
evening.

Though his sight ain't so clear anymore, him comin' up on
ninety-five here perty soon, Mathias quietly chuckles when he

sometimes thinks he can tell which family of Yoders, Lapps, or Kings a proud steed belongs to. He can tell, he says, by the rhythm of the horse's hooves on the pavement. 'Course, now, his unmarried daughter, who lives with him and comes out ev'ry so often, checkin' to see if'n he needs some water to wet his whistle, or maybe some hot coffee to warm him up, well . . . she doesn't believe a word of it. "Don't try 'n' fool me, Dat," she'll say, her hands on her stout hips. "Ain't no way a body can tell one horse from another by its trottin'." With that, she turns and goes back inside, leaving him there alone on the porch. Which is just the way he likes it, 'specially come night-fall.

Alone. Where he can think back to his own months of courtin', ever so long ago that he needs the aid of his harmonica, the stillness of the night, and the sound of the *clip-clopping* to ease his memory back to former days, growin' up here on Grasshopper Level, meetin' and marryin' one of the pertiest girls God ever made. His precious bride—Mattie Sue—long gone, over twenty years now. Still, it seems like just yesterday he promised to "nevermore depart from her," vowin' before the Amish bishop and the many witnesses gathered in the house that he would care for her and cherish her, until the dear God would again separate them one from the other, in death.

Care for and cherish his Mattie, he had. 'Specially her last few years on God's green earth, when her tiny body was so pained she couldn't walk a'tall. But Mathias saw to it that Mattie got ev'ry place she wanted to go, carryin' her in his big, strong arms from one room to 'nother as if she were a small child. He took her for rides in the carriage on warm nights, her smellin' for all the world like lilies of the valley, her favorite scent. They rode round and round the same route he'd taken when first courtin' her. My, oh my, how she loved the sights of evening. Her hearing had given out years before, due to a bad stroke, but she made up for the loss by lookin' hard at sky and trees, and the quilt patterns in the farmland, just a-soakin' up the countryside with her shining blue eyes.

Well, tonight he certainly hoped the young men out courtin' had the gut sense to find and marry *their* sweetheart girls, just as he had so many years ago. So with fond memories, he plays his music, tears a-rollin' down his face. He hopes Mattie's listening, and surely she is, close as they'd always been. No question in his mind the Good Lord will see to it that Mattie Sue hears a snatch or two of her beloved's heartfelt playin'.

In between songs, just now, he thinks he recognizes the sound of the King boy's horse. Jah, leanin' his ear hard at the road, he listens, knowing 'tis young Levi out there prob'ly, driving his best mare, impressin' that young Cottrell girl. Word has it Lyddie and Levi are seein' a lot of each other, since just last spring. There's even talk that the two are planning on tyin' the knot 'fore too long. And from what Mathias knows of Levi, ain't a more compassionate, spirited young man round here. As for Lydia, well, her parents did a wonderful-gut job of raisin' her in the faith—in the fear of the Lord—even if they *were* a tad more liberal, leanin' in the direction of them New Order folk.

But that's all right. He wishes Lyddie a lifetime of happiness with her Levi. For goodness' sake, Lyddie deserves a gut young man. My, my, but she's gone through hard times for such a young one. Losin' first her father to a terrible accident, then her mamma to a failed heart just last year. Then havin' to adjust to outsiders—fancy English folk—comin' in and taking over as guardians. Just ain't the way you'd expect things to turn out for a family with hearts of pure gold.

Quickly, he puts the harmonica back in his mouth, breathing deeply, then starts to play his best song for Lyddie. Poor, dear girl . . .

Why, he could name off a whole list of downright puzzlin' things, painful things, too, that there just ain't answers for. He's seen such things throughout all his life. Still, he's steadfast, unmovable in his beliefs, trustin' the Good Lord. Wouldn't ever consider wearin' a chip on his shoulder against the Almighty.

He puffs ever so hard into his harmonica, with a prayer in his heart that the couples a-courtin' on his road might find the peace of the Savior. If'n they haven't already done that most holy thing—baptism into the church. Some of them, he fears, have put off doin' so, seeking after things uppermost on their young minds: a little smoochin', getting married, and bearin' young ones in a matter of time. Ach, he knows they'll grow wiser with the years. Same as he did.

Wiser and stronger in the faith of their fathers . . .

So he rocks in his chair and plays at twilight, wishin' them well, each and ev'ry one . . . offering up his tunes. 'Tis the least ol' Mathias can do, as the sun sinks low, behind Grasshopper Level.

Then along 'bout bedtime, when he knows he oughta get up from his comfortable hickory rocker and head back into the house, 'bout that time, he hears the sound of another horse and carriage, movin' ever so slowly down the road. Tuning his ear to the horse's rhythm, he finds it somewhat familiar, but . . . no, he can't seem to put his finger on just whose horse *this* one might be. But it's slowing down, all the same . . . pausing and stopping in front of his old farmhouse.

Eyes seeing ever so clearly now, he stops playin' his music. "Well, now, who's this?" he whispers into the night.

◆

When his daughter came to help him indoors, she noticed his harmonica lyin' beneath the hickory rocker. "Dat," she whispered, " 'tis time to call it a day."

He said not a word but wore a smile on his wrinkled face, eyes closed now, head slumped to his chest. Bending low, she picked up the beloved instrument, a strange and delicate sweetness of lily of the valley all round him.

A Virtuous Woman

The easy, gentle, and sloping path . . . is not the path of true virtue.
It demands a rough and thorny road.

—Michel de Montaigne

Sarah awakened at her usual early-morning hour, well before five o'clock. Not only must she cook breakfast and make sack lunches for Bryan, Lydia, and the younger children, there were surely a number of e-mail messages to check on before she left the house for a busy morning at the real estate office near downtown Lancaster.

First things first. She scurried down the narrow hallway to Caleb's bedroom, firmly knocking on the door. "Caleb! Are you up?"

"Jah, and Josiah is, too," her nephew called through the door. "Denki, Aunt Sarah."

The cows were waiting to be milked, as they were twice daily. Thankfully, Caleb, Josiah, and, most of the time, Bryan handled *that* particular outside chore. Now she must focus on getting Lydia off to school, where, now that mornings were cooler, her seventeen-year-old niece—schoolteacher and soon-to-be-bride—must arrive at the one-room school long before her students to start a fire in the wood stove. "I still remember goin' to a chilly schoolhouse when I was a girl and shiverin' all through morning lessons," Lyddie had told her recently. "Doesn't make for gut learnin', really."

Bryan was up now, tossing clean clothes into his suitcase for a short trip to Boston. He planned to leave immediately following breakfast. "The earlier I can get away, the sooner I'll return," he said with a gentle kiss and fierce hug.

Finally, Caleb, Anna Mae, Josiah, and Hannah had to leave for Peach Lane School in ample time to walk to the one-room school. Caleb, the oldest of the school-aged children, had declared yesterday, "There's no sense us ridin' with you, Aunt Sarah, when the walkin' will do us all gut!" To which Anna Mae piped up, "Jah, and besides, we ride to church in a *car* on Sundays, so maybe we oughta walk or take the horse and buggy everywhere else durin' the week."

Atonement? Sarah wondered if that's what Anna Mae had in mind, but she didn't dwell on it. There was much to do today. The large wicker basket of mending had begun to pile up so high the clothes in question had spilled onto the laundry room floor, making it difficult to know which clothes were clean and in need of repair and which were merely soiled, in need of laundering.

Hannah, an exceptionally tall seven-year-old, was sprouting up fast, already wearing Anna Mae's hand-me-downs, though fairly swimming in them. Josiah, almost nine, was not only growing up but out, as well.

"The youngest always get the short end of things," Lyddie told Sarah the other day, when Hannah was complaining about the length of her sleeves and drooping hemline. "If I have some extra time, maybe I can sew some new dresses and aprons for her."

"Oh, Lyddie, I can't let you do that," Sarah had insisted. Lyddie, after all, was maxed out with teaching duties, sewing a solid blue dress and white organdy cape and apron for her wedding, and organizing several key women—close friends of the family—to prepare food for the reception at the church banquet hall, enough to feed two hundred or more guests.

Sarah, too, had been assisting Lyddie with various aspects of the wedding: addressing the handwritten invitations—thirty or more each night—assigning the reception menu of cold cuts, cheeses, home-baked breads of all kinds, fresh vegetables and fruit, and desserts—pies, cakes, and cookies—to several different women in the neighborhood. Sarah would bake the wedding cake, of course, and supply the fruit punch.

On the home front, she had been trying to keep her head above water, which was becoming a losing battle. Just last evening, she and Bryan had talked over the idea of dividing up more of the chores between the two of them, but Bryan was busy with the duties of the main breadwinner of the family, and Sarah felt strongly that it was *her* responsibility to keep the children clean and in well-mended clothing, cook the meals, keep her hand in the real estate business, and put smiles on everyone's faces. In short, be "super-aunt-mom."

After many months of juggling duties, including household tasks and farm chores, she was beginning to wonder how the virtuous woman described in Proverbs had managed to do so much. When it came to sewing skills, Sarah scarcely had any, let alone the talent to create "coverings of tapestry . . . and fine

213

linen." Mending was easy enough if she could consistently set aside part of a morning each week to do so, but lately she found herself going and coming, literally running in circles between home duties and work expectations.

What can I eliminate from my schedule? she wondered as she greased her hands and began to knead the bread dough.

Then, glancing at the calendar hanging from the cellar door, she noted that Lyddie had scribbled something on today's date—a work frolic at Miriam Esh's place. "Go 'n' watch them put up vegetables and whatnot," Lyddie had urged Sarah last week. "You'll catch on quick as a wink."

Sarah had been tempted to go and learn the art of preserving fruits and vegetables from the hands of the experts, her own Amish neighbors and many of the children's church friends. But the manager of the real estate office, where she worked, had called a meeting for nine o'clock this morning. She would scarcely have enough time to bake two loaves of bread, clean the kitchen thoroughly, make a slight dent in the mending, and shower and dress in her most professional attire. So much for a canning lesson at Miriam's.

She sighed. *Just as well.* Sometimes she thought it best to keep her distance, to some extent, from the many Plain women of the community. She and Bryan had no plans to surrender their "fancy" life, as Lyddie often referred to their lifestyle. "No sense kiddin' anyone, jah?" Lyddie would say, her serious look soon turning to a grin.

Lydia was her mother's perceptive oldest offspring. She was also Sarah's salvation. She often thought of her niece in that way—the epitome of liberator. Lyddie, after all, had won her heart less than a year ago, having "prayed her into the household." The delightful young woman was a bundle of energy, both physically and spiritually. Some days Sarah wondered what she might have done without Lyddie to confer with, to talk through Plain issues that were still very foreign . . . to help her make the transition from distant aunt to stepmother and legal guardian. With Lyddie's wedding only a few weeks away, Sarah was beginning to miss her "right arm," so to speak, which was precisely what Lyddie had become.

"The Lord will provide for all your needs—body, mind, and spirit. Don't doubt it," Lyddie assured her with a disarming twinkle in her golden-brown eyes. "Besides that, I'll be just down the road, less than a mile. You can always call me up or drive over for a visit. Anytime."

"We'll manage somehow, but that's not to say we won't miss you terribly. All of us will," Sarah had replied.

Now she set about cooking an enormous breakfast, placing a bowl of fresh fruit on the table—raspberries, grapes, and sliced oranges. All the while she thought of the Scripture passages her husband had read to the children last night before bedtime. Gladly, they had continued to observe "evening prayers" not only for the children's sake, but for their own. Bryan, a fairly new Christian, and Sarah, having even more recently embraced the faith, were eagerly growing in the knowledge of God's Word. In many ways, they enjoyed much of the Plain family rituals pertaining to the study of the Bible. Sarah especially relished her morning talks with God. Her deceased sister had acquired this joyful habit, too, as revealed in Ivy's personal journals. Thanks to Lyddie, Sarah had been privileged to read nearly all of her sister's letters and diary entries. A blessing in more ways than she could enumerate, because

Ivy and her husband had also come to the Plain community after having lived and experienced a modern way of life. Just as Sarah and Bryan had, though for completely different reasons.

Thinking back to the struggles—how, in fact, her present existence had come to be—she was grateful for the opportunity to make a difference in her sister's orphaned children's lives. The irony was that Lydia, Caleb, Anna Mae, Josiah, and little Hannah had, indeed, altered the course of *her* life . . . and for the better. As much as she wished to be a loving wife and mother figure, she also wanted to manage effectively the household God had ordained for her.

Former friends and colleagues back in Oregon had been shocked at her declaration last winter that she was moving to Pennsylvania Amish country to raise her nieces and nephews. And she had married her college boyfriend, Bryan Ford, on top of everything else. "What's happened to Sarah Cain?" the whispers flitted from one end of the real estate office to the other. "How will a modern businesswoman fit in?"

Fitting in *had* been challenging. Still was. But it wasn't as though she'd had to revolutionize her entire lifestyle. Thankfully, she enjoyed her collection of classical CDs and watched the fluctuating stock market with interest on her and Bryan's TV. The "one-eyed monster," as the children referred to it, was confined to their bedroom. Her magazine subscriptions continued to find their way to her each month, and her cell phone was in use when necessary, not to mention a laptop computer with its faxing and e-mailing capabilities. Plain dressing had never been part of the plan for either her or Bryan; neither was abandoning their nice cars.

She sometimes wondered how the children viewed her and Bryan. As outsiders? Certainly not "seekers," in the sense that they were interested in church membership among the People. Did her nieces and nephews suspect her to be a part-time mother figure, planning her getaway the minute they were married and on their own?

Nothing could be further from the truth. Having fallen in love with Ivy's precious offspring, Sarah had never considered abandoning the family that had become hers in every way. And Bryan, *he* was equally smitten with the whole lot of them, eager to add to the family unit whenever the Lord chose to bless them with another child.

"Who do you know that sews for pay in the area?" Sarah asked Lyddie as they all sat down at breakfast.

"Plenty of women do," Lyddie replied. "There's a notice posted in the church entrance hall. I'll check on that for ya . . . give Preacher Esh a call."

Sarah glanced at the children, lined up on either side of the table, looking bright-eyed and happy. "I would gladly pay someone to sew for Hannah and Josiah. And anyone else in the family for that matter."

Bryan was in total agreement, nodding his head. "Well, honey, maybe the boys won't mind if *I* had some clothes sewn for me, too."

Josiah jumped on the comment, leaning over his plate as he spoke. "*You*, Uncle Bryan? Are you gonna wear Plain clothes like Caleb and me?"

Sarah intervened. "Uncle Bryan's pulling your leg."

Josiah lifted the tablecloth and looked under the table.

"My leg's fine . . . ain't bein' pulled on a'tall!"

"*Isn't*," said Lyddie. "Ain't isn't a word . . . remember?"

But Josiah was still looking down at his leg, playing along with Sarah. "I'm waitin' for Uncle Bryan to tug on my leg."

Sarah, aware of the time, folded her hands, waiting for her husband to lead in a prayer of blessing over the food. "We'll talk after the prayer," she said, and immediately a hush fell over the kitchen.

Sarah wrapped things up at the real estate office a half hour or so before the children began their trek home from school. She concluded her phone call with an interested client and said good-bye to the receptionist, frustrated that she hadn't been able to "nail the deal."

Tomorrow or the weekend, she thought, hoping she'd have time to phone back later.

When she arrived home, Lyddie was talking on the phone to Preacher Esh, gathering information about a seamstress.

"I think I've heard of this woman," Lyddie said, after she hung up. She studied the piece of paper, where she'd written the name and phone number. "Preacher Esh says he knows both her and her husband. They're conservative Mennonites—'good, solid Christian folk,' who live not far from Hickory Hollow." Lyddie handed the information to her.

"Thanks for your help." Then, picking up the phone, she dialed the number for a Mrs. Katie Fisher.

The phone rang twice, then—"Hullo . . . Fishers."

"May I speak to Katie, please?"

"This is she."

"My name is Sarah Ford. I live near Strasburg . . . and I'm calling about my young niece and nephew, who need traditional Amish clothing sewn for them."

"May I ask how you got my name?"

Sarah quickly filled her in about the notice posted at Lyddie's church. "Preacher Esh highly recommended you."

"Jah, I know Brother Esh well . . . through my husband," the woman said. "And I do happen to have some time this week. When wouldja like to come over?"

Sarah decided on tomorrow afternoon, which was ideal. Both Hannah and Josiah would have something new to wear—that actually fit—for their big sister's wedding. "I'll look forward to meeting you tomorrow."

"Please bring the children along when you come."

"Oh yes, of course I will." She was glad Katie Fisher had thought of reminding her of that important detail. Face flushed with embarrassment, she hurried back to the kitchen to prepare supper. Knowing she could ease Lyddie's burden somewhat by her not having to sew after all made Sarah feel lighter. Even joyful. Perhaps she'd find time to dive into the mending basket this evening, after supper and evening prayers, after addressing the rest of the wedding invitations with Lyddie, after making another phone call to her client . . . once everyone was tucked into bed.

Sarah washed some lettuce, cucumbers, carrots, and tomatoes for a vegetable salad, while Lyddie graded papers at the kitchen table. As she worked, she wondered about the secret behind Martha Stewart's success. Was part of it the fact that the amazing woman demonstrated—each time she was in front of a TV camera, every time she wrote a book or a magazine article—her ability to extend part of herself to others? Wasn't that, after all, the basis of hospitality, offering oneself completely?

Looking up from her stack of work, Lyddie offered to help peel potatoes, "when I'm finished grading papers."

Instantly, Sarah felt guilty. "You have so much to do, Lyddie. Just leave all the cooking to me tonight. I insist."

"Honestly, I don't mind, Aunt Sarah."

She smiled. "I know you don't, which is precisely what makes you so special."

At that, Lyddie rose from the table and hurried across the room to Sarah. She planted a kiss on her cheek. "I'll go 'n' find Anna Mae. 'Tis time she helps out a bit more in the kitchen."

Sarah had been thinking the same thing. "Anna Mae's a good candidate for potato peeling," she said.

"And don't ever let her talk you out of inside chores. Anna Mae can be testy that way," Lyddie said over her shoulder, heading outside to find her younger sister.

Sarah laughed softly, thinking of her friends out west. If they could see her now . . .

"After school tomorrow I'll pick up you and Josiah," Sarah told Hannah just before supper. "Caleb and Anna Mae can ride home in the buggy with Lyddie if they like."

Hannah's eyes lit up. "Where're Josiah and me goin'?"

"Josiah and *I*," Lyddie corrected as she set the table.

Sarah leaned down and kissed Hannah's little head. "You and your brother are going to have some new clothes made."

That brought a grin to Hannah's face. "Are ya sayin' I won't hafta wear Anna Mae's clothes no more?"

"*Anymore*," Lyddie said.

"Yes, that's exactly what it means." Sarah pointed to the sink, where Hannah quickly went to wash her hands.

"Ach, I can't wait!" Hannah said.

Sarah was pleased with the little girl's response, hoping that Josiah, when he and Caleb came in from milking, might feel equally happy.

The news quickly found its way to Josiah's ears. Hannah must have filled him in while Sarah and Lyddie carried serving dishes to the table. Less than two seconds passed after the "amen" was said, and Josiah, now scowling, announced to all of them, "I hope I won't hafta strip naked tomorrow!"

"Well, for goodness' sake, Josiah!" reprimanded Lyddie.

Sarah stifled a smile. "Why would you think you'd have to remove your old clothes to be measured for new ones?"

"That's what my friend Ezra has to do when *he* gets new clothes," Josiah said.

"I can tell you right now, you have nothing to worry about." She passed the potatoes around to Caleb, then the chicken gravy.

"Who knows *what* the seamstress will do?" Caleb piped up, his voice deeper than Sarah had ever heard it.

Josiah's eyes grew wide. "Ach, what's Caleb sayin'?"

Sarah spoke directly to Caleb. "Why are you trying to frighten your brother?"

The older boy's face was even more solemn than before. "Do you have any idea who you're goin' to . . . to have clothes sewn for this family?"

Sarah gave Caleb a sidewise glance, frowning. "I think you'd better say what's on your mind."

The young teenager's eyes narrowed a bit, and he leaned forward at the table. "Some of my older friends have heard tell of Katie and her husband—Daniel Fisher—a man who disappeared years ago at sea and was passed off as dead for a gut five years."

"What on earth are you talking 'bout?" Lyddie spoke up.

"Just listen. Katie Fisher is a shunned woman, an outcast in her community."

"Maybe so, but Preacher Esh never would've suggested her to Aunt Sarah if he thought there was a problem," Lyddie said. "Besides, the way one church district disciplines a member has nothing to do with another's treatment of that person, jah?"

Sarah wondered about the mysterious Daniel Fisher. Why hadn't Lyddie heard any of this? "Why was the woman shunned in the first place?" she asked.

Caleb shrugged. "Don't know for sure, really. Word has it she upped and jilted the bishop she was s'posed to marry, and he put a harsh shunning on her. After that, she went searchin' for her birth mother, leavin' behind the People, only to come back and join the Mennonites."

Anna Mae had a question. "What happened to the man who almost drowned?"

"Katie married *him* instead of the bishop," said Caleb.

Josiah clapped his hands with glee. "Sounds like a fish story to me—Jonah and the whale!"

Sarah got things calmed things down by passing the mashed potatoes and gravy around a second time.

Then Lyddie said, "Preacher Esh told me that Katie Fisher and her husband are solid Christians, so I'm goin' to take *his* word over all of yours."

"Suit yourself," Caleb said glibly. "But don't say I didn't warn you."

Josiah stared nervously at the puddle of gravy in the middle of his potatoes. "Do I hafta go? I can make do with my old clothes."

Sarah reached across the table and touched his hand. "I think you'd much prefer the britches Mrs. Fisher sews for you than the ones *I* could make." That brought a smile to the boy's face, and the subject was dropped.

Once the children were settled into bed, however, the topic surfaced again. Sarah and Lyddie were working together at the kitchen table, Sarah addressing invitations as fast and as neatly as possible and Lyddie setting in the sleeves of her wedding dress by hand.

"What type of sin would cause an Amishwoman to be shunned?" Sarah had heard very little about the practice, and due to Caleb's comments at supper, she was quite curious.

"Amongst the Old Order there are a gut many things that can prompt church discipline for a woman," Lyddie explained. "Too short a hemline, for one; cutting or curling her hair, dating or marryin' an outsider, ownin' a television or a car . . ." At the mention of televisions and cars, Lyddie turned a bit sheepish. "But my church—the New Order fellowship of believers—doesn't embrace shunning practices," she added quickly. "Still, we're very strict 'bout other things."

Lyddie's church required the utmost of holiness in daily living—modesty of dress, godly speech, and purity of deed. But they also embraced wholeheartedly the assurance of salvation, through faith in Jesus Christ, just as Sarah and Bryan did.

"Some of the shunning practices in Lancaster County are more severe than you'd think. Heartbreaking, really. But, then, some are ever so lenient, too. All depends on the bishop and the church."

"Marrying a Mennonite man—if you were raised Amish— would that be a reason to be shunned?" she asked, trying to piece the puzzle together.

"If the person has been baptized into the Old Order church, jah, the shun . . . for sure and for certain."

Sarah found Lyddie's answer to be curious. Just who *was* the Mennonite seamstress named Katie Fisher?

Before retiring for the night, Sarah read her Bible, turning to the second chapter of First Thessalonians, reading verses six through eight aloud. " 'As apostles of Christ we could have been a burden to you, but we were gentle among you, like a mother caring for her little children. We loved you so much that we were delighted to share with you not only the gospel of God but our lives as well, because you had become so dear to us.' "

She marveled at the beauty of the words, this tender encouragement written by the apostle Paul. Would she remember them tomorrow? She sighed sleepily, feeling somewhat convicted—a tug at her very soul. Motherhood required sacrifice, every ounce of energy and ingenuity she had to offer.

She was so weary. . . .

In her mind's eye, she was a young girl gathering seashells with her father, washing the clinging, wet sand from her fingers, tracing the smoothness of the shell, enjoying its fragile texture—the eye-catching shape—seeing the tinge of color. All the while, her father shared not only his faith with her, but his very life. Yet all this required an interlude from the stroll along the shoreline. *"Stop for a moment, and take time to cherish the treasure,"* her father's words came back to her.

Yes, this thing she must do daily as wife, mother/aunt, businesswoman, and new Christian. *Cherish the treasure . . .*

The distant echo of her father's words touched her profoundly. Even now she lay, weary and anxious, missing Bryan, praying she could manage well without Lyddie, wanting to meet the needs of Caleb, Anna Mae, Josiah, and Hannah. Wishing . . . no, *longing* to be God's kind of woman.

Keeping things simple was the key to peace and happiness. Wasn't it? But how, with such a complicated, busy life? Must she quit working, give up her professional job she'd worked so hard to carve out for herself?

Not possessing the answer, she gave in to sleep.

Long before the alarm sounded the next morning, Sarah

awakened, in tune to the schedule of her days. She stretched, reaching for Bryan. Finding only his pillow, she quickly recalled that her husband was in Boston.

She yawned and sat up. If she hurried she could mend clothes, finish addressing Lyddie and Levi's wedding invitations, bake two loaves of oatmeal bread, have her morning talk with the Lord, and bathe and dress for the day before it was time to prepare another big breakfast for the children.

I'll pace myself better today, she thought with determination. *And I'll cherish the treasure.*

Slipping into her bathrobe, she headed for the hallway, deciding to let Caleb and Josiah sleep another half hour. It was still very early. She tiptoed down the steps to the laundry room and the mending basket, her thoughts on the shunned woman, the seamstress Lyddie had found for her. Unsure why, Sarah could scarcely wait to meet Katie Fisher.

◆

Sarah did not allow herself to sit down to eat lunch, though running around during a meal was discouraged, even frowned upon, by health experts. She took small bites of her roast beef sandwich, then scanned her e-mail messages on the laptop computer while standing, checking on messages from the office, returning phone calls, and finishing up with a client, promising to show him a good selection of homes this Saturday when Bryan would be home again and could hold down the fort.

Between additional bites, she put a load of laundry in the

washing machine, even though Amish wash day was two days past. She swept the floors in the kitchen and utility room, took out a large roast to thaw—how convenient it would be to have a microwave again!—then hurried to gather up the wedding invitations, putting stamps on each one, then double-checking the addresses and the return address.

By the time the invitations were sufficiently stuffed into the mailbox for afternoon pickup, the washing had run its final rinse-and-dry cycle. Sarah tossed the damp clothing into the wide wicker basket, most having been newly mended before dawn this morning, and though it was after noon, she didn't mind hanging the clothes out to dry, the day being warm. Perfect for drying clothes. Prying neighbors, who could see the clothesline from their homes, might wonder why she'd waited so late in the day, or why she'd done some washing on a Wednesday in the first place. But, truly, what they thought didn't bother her. Sarah was focused on cherishing the treasure of today, of giving herself away for the sake of five precious young people. Her own flesh-and-blood family. Her God-given duty.

◆

Katie Fisher's home lay deep in the Amish farming community southwest of the village of Intercourse by a few miles, off Cattail Road. Sarah chose to take the back way, the thin road curving ahead of her, oak trees moving not a limb as the sun filtered its light through leaves of rusty reds, sky as wide as a blue platter. With the harvest nearly complete, only a few farmers were left working, the fields having surrendered up their bounty.

Hannah and Josiah sat in the backseat of the car, chattering about their day at school. Sarah listened in only when Lyddie's name came up, concerning the lessons taught to the students.

"We learned 'bout sharin' today at school," Josiah said. "We *needed* to."

"Oh?" Sarah replied, wondering what the motivation for *that* lesson might have been.

"Jah, some of the boys were mean to the girls," Hannah volunteered quickly.

Josiah set the record straight. "That's what *you* say!"

"Well, the boys weren't nice, and you know it," Hannah insisted.

"Now, children," Sarah broke in. "Did your teacher help with the situation?"

"Jah, Lyddie taught all of us 'bout sharing . . . and she read from the Bible on the Golden Rule," Hannah said.

"Lyddie made us recite out loud," Josiah said.

Sarah saw, by looking in her rearview mirror, that Josiah was eyeballing his sister. "Did *each* of you learn a good lesson?" she probed.

Josiah was quick to say *he* did.

"What about you, Hannah?" she asked.

"Lyddie's a right gut teacher, Aunt Sarah. We'll miss her when she's married," Hannah said. "We learn ever so much from her, 'cause she loves us so."

"Who's gonna teach us after Lyddie's married, do ya think?" Josiah asked.

228

"We'll pray about your new teacher. The Lord already knows who she will be," Sarah reassured them.

Josiah and Hannah settled down a bit, and Josiah stopped staring at his sister.

Because she loves us so . . .

Sarah had to smile, even in spite of the children's spat. She, like Lyddie, truly loved these children. Enough to quit her job and be a stay-at-home mom. Yes, she would relinquish her career as a real estate agent, at least for this season of her life. Bryan would be in perfect agreement, she knew.

◆

Finding the correct address, Sarah parked the car at the curb, in front of the clapboard bungalow. Bright yellow marigolds bloomed brightly along a brick walkway that led to the front door, and on the porch there was an inviting swing for two. Crimson geraniums, protected by the roof, still flourished alongside several wicker chairs.

Katie Fisher has a green thumb, she decided.

"Please be on your best behavior," she said to Hannah and Josiah before getting out of the car.

"We will, Aunt Sarah," Hannah promised.

Josiah nodded his head, opening his car door. "Jah . . ."

Katie Fisher opened the front door and stepped onto the porch, wearing a high-necked, long yellow dress with miniature flowers dancing through the fabric. Her auburn hair was parted down the middle, pulled back in a soft bun at the back of her neck, with a small white head covering.

Together, Sarah and the children walked up the flower-lined walkway to the neat little house. "Hello," Sarah said, introducing herself. "I phoned yesterday."

The young woman stood at the top of the porch steps, stooping low to greet the children. "Well, now, who's this?" Katie Fisher said, apparently delighted.

"This is my niece Hannah and my nephew Josiah," Sarah said.

"I'm ever so glad to meet you. My name is Katie Fisher. Please, won'tcha come inside?" A smile lit up her face.

"Denki," Hannah said. Josiah said nothing.

The kitchen smelled of freshly baked cinnamon rolls, and Katie offered the sweet treats on an oval platter. "Go ahead and sit at the table, if you like," she said, pulling a chair out for Hannah.

Small, but cozy, the room was sunny and bright with bold accents—an open area of shelving displayed mismatched sets of bright green and yellow coffee mugs and teacups and saucers. A rounded vintage toaster caught her eye on the counter, as did the glass salt-and-pepper shakers sporting red tops. A small stack of green-and-white-checked cloth napkins lay near a Mason jar filled with pink wild flowers. In one corner, Sarah spotted what must have been two guitar cases, matching ones. For a "conservative Mennonite," as Preacher Esh had referred to Katie Fisher, her kitchen was surprisingly eye-catching and vibrant with color.

"How many dresses do ya want sewn for Hannah?" Katie asked.

"Let's make it three, while we're at it."

Katie nodded. "And Josiah . . . he needs trousers and forgut shirts?"

"Two pairs of pants and two dress shirts," replied Sarah.

As they discussed the traditional fabric and colors for the children's new clothes, Katie commented that she would keep a running tally on the cost of the fabric, sewing notions, and, of course, her time. "But, don't worry, you can afford *me*," she said with a smile.

After washing her hands, Hannah was first, standing on a chair while Katie measured her from shoulders to waistline, and waist to hem, shoulder to wrist, around the bodice, waist, and hips, and across her shoulders. "You're a quiet one," Katie said when she was finished.

Hannah smiled, showing a front tooth missing.

"She's a sweet girl, too," Sarah said, motioning now for Josiah, whose face had turned suddenly white. "Are you all right?"

"I . . . uh," he stuttered. "I'm not feelin' so gut just now."

Katie's smile faded. "He can go out and sit on the porch swing a bit. The fresh air will help, maybe."

"I'll go with him," Hannah said, following her brother.

Sarah went quickly to the porch, as well. "Are you sick?" she asked Josiah.

"Don't know."

She thought he might be bashful. "Relax here with Hannah, and I'll check on you in a few minutes."

Eager to get better acquainted with Katie, she headed back to the kitchen. "I think Josiah may be feeling awkward," she explained.

"Jah, I 'spect so, bein' outnumbered by us women." Katie

put some water on to boil. "Wouldja care for some tea?"

"Sounds lovely. Thanks."

They talked for a while about the nice weather, the exceptionally blue skies, the harvest nearly past. Ordinary things.

Then, cautiously Katie said, "Your niece and nephew wear traditional Amish clothing, yet you are English. Am I right?" Her eyes were bright with interest.

Sarah laughed softly. "It's quite a long story . . . unbelievable, too."

"A wonderful-gut story, I 'spect?"

"Most people raise an eyebrow at a non-Amishwoman and her husband taking on a houseful of youngsters."

"Well, my friend Mary, who's Old Order, did just that," Katie volunteered. "And I . . . well, I came mighty close to doin' the same thing some months before Mary did."

"Really?" Sarah was all ears. "What happened?"

"I couldn't—didn't—go through with . . . marryin' the widower."

"A widower with several children?" Sarah didn't want to press for more than Katie wished to offer. She would be cautious, as warm and open as this woman was, sitting across the table from her.

"Five dear ones," said Katie.

"Five?" Her heart leaped with empathy. "That's how many nieces and nephews I have custody of, at least until the oldest girl is married . . . not long from now."

Eyes glistening, Katie nodded. "Ach, how I loved those children." She paused. "But I just couldn't marry their father, the bishop."

Sarah was caught off guard for a moment. What had Caleb

said about a harsh shunning imposed by a jilted bishop? Dared she inquire?

Delicately, they talked around the burning questions. Sarah shared a bit more of her past, how she'd actually come to live in Lancaster County and had a change of heart, turning from a materialistic businesswoman to guardian for her deceased sister's children.

Katie must have felt at ease enough to reciprocate, telling her own story, weaving a fascinating tale of heartbreak and betrayal. An English baby orphaned, then adopted by Amish parents, a girl kept in the dark about "the secret" until the eve of her wedding to an older man—a widower bishop with five young children. When she finished, she sighed deeply.

Having registered the pain of Katie's years, Sarah considered it an honor to sip tea and nibble on cinnamon rolls with the shunned and courageous woman. And, continuing to pour out her heart, she discovered that her life and Katie's had run somewhat parallel, quite astonishingly, though Sarah had not been adopted or grown up in an Amish home. Nonetheless, both women had yearned for what was out of their reach— beyond the boundaries—only to find futility when they'd pushed the limits. "The world holds no attraction for me," Sarah said at last.

"Jah, such emptiness there is," Katie agreed.

"Receiving the phone call from Lyddie . . . learning that my sister had died was actually the beginning of a better, more joyful life."

"I believe God's grace caught up with you," Katie said softly.

The Mennonite woman had a unique way of putting

things. In every way, Sarah liked Katie. "I guess I'd better check on Josiah," she said glancing at the clock. She got up and went to the porch. "How are you feeling now?" She slipped her hand under her nephew's bangs.

He looked up at her. "I thought I might faint, is all."

Katie came out and sat in one of the wicker chairs, across from Josiah. "I sew for quite a few boys your age," she said. "I thought if you knew that, you might be feelin' better 'bout things."

Josiah's eyes nearly popped out. "Do ya sew for a boy named Ezra Hess?"

"Why, no, I don't. But I can tell ya who does."

Josiah's eyes blinked much too fast.

Katie wore a clever smile. "Ezra's *mamma* makes all his clothes, 'least that's my understanding."

Josiah's nose wrinkled. "That's odd," he mumbled.

"Why's that?" Katie prodded.

He shook his head. "I best not be sayin'."

Sarah asked, "Could it be that you're mistaken about . . . well, you know what?"

Josiah surely knew what she was talking about, that Ezra Hess had to take off his clothes to be measured. "Mistaken . . . jah, prob'ly so," he admitted. "Ezra must be pullin' my leg like Uncle Bryan does." His face relaxed then and a smile appeared.

Hannah was giggling now.

" 'Tis a family joke, jah?" Katie wore a knowing grin.

Reaching over, Sarah tickled Josiah under the arm. "I think you're feeling much better, aren't you?"

He sat up straight, grinning. "If Ezra can do this, so can I."

And with that, he stood up and led Hannah, Katie, and Sarah back into the house.

With both children measured for new clothes, Sarah was reluctant to leave the peaceful abode. And Katie's company. "You and your husband must come for supper sometime," she said. "Then you can meet the rest of the family."

"And maybe she can come to Lyddie's and Levi's wedding," Josiah said out of the blue.

"Levi?" said Katie, eyes sparkling. "Is it Levi King, by any chance?"

Sarah said it was. "Do you know him?"

"My husband works with Levi's cousin . . . in fact, he's thinkin' of offering Levi a job."

"Is that so?" Sarah was amazed at this connection. "We'll send you an invitation to the wedding."

Katie nodded. "I'd like that, truly I would."

"You can see Josiah and me in our new clothes if you come," Hannah spoke up.

"I surely will," Katie said, leaning down to pat Hannah's hand. She accompanied them to the front door, turning to Sarah as she did. "Your niece and nephew are ever so adorable. What a pleasant afternoon."

"Thanks for everything." Sarah extended her hand to Katie.

"I feel like I've known you forever," Katie said, accepting the handshake and squeezing her hand gently.

Sarah agreed. "God knew I needed a friend."

"The Lord has ways of bringin' folk together."

Thanks, Lord, she thought. Saying their good-byes, Sarah and the children headed down the quaint brick walkway to the car.

Katie followed them, waiting while Sarah helped the children into the backseat. "I'll be callin' you next week, prob'ly. Won't take too long to sew up the clothes."

Turning, Sarah smiled back at Katie. "You're a godsend . . . absolutely." *In more ways than one,* she thought.

"Well, the Lord bless you and your family."

"God bless *you,* Katie."

Katie's face was aglow as she stood in the yard, waving to all of them. "Safe home!" she called.

As Sarah drove away she caught herself staring in the rear-view mirror, watching wistfully until the image of the Mennonite woman in flowing yellow dress and white prayer cap—hiding some but not all of Katie's beautiful red hair—was no longer visible.

O suns and skies and clouds of June,
  And flowers of June together,
  Ye cannot rival for one hour
  October's bright blue weather.

—Helen Hunt Jackson

$\mathcal{T}$o readers for whom *October Song* has been the first Beverly Lewis novel they have read, the following pages will introduce you to her preceding novels on which the stories in *October Song* are based.

❧❧❧❧❧

For further information on particular books or suggestions for obtaining copies, please visit the Bethany House Publishers Web site (www.bethanyhouse.com) or call 1-800-328-6109.

THE HERITAGE OF
LANCASTER COUNTY

Beverly Lewis's
Bestselling Introduction
to Christian Fiction
Readers!

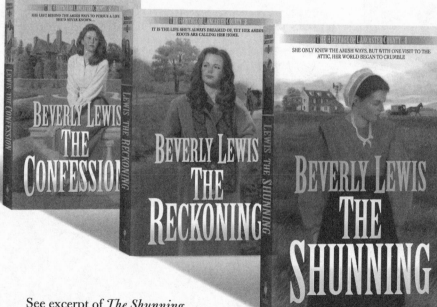

See excerpt of *The Shunning*
on page 251.

THE HERITAGE OF LANCASTER COUNTY

AN EMOTIONAL AND POIGNANT TRILOGY that marked the entrance of a new voice into the world of Christian novelists. Set in the author's beloved Lancaster County, each story includes issues of family, belonging, and community along with fascinating and authentic glimpses into Amish life.

In the quiet Amish community of Hickory Hollow, Pennsylvania, time stands still while cherished traditions and heartfelt beliefs flourish. But a buried secret could shatter the tranquility its inhabitants have grown to love.

When Katie Lapp stumbles upon a satin infant gown in the dusty letter trunk of her parents' attic, she knows it holds a story she must discover. Why else would her Amish mother, a plain and simple woman who embraces the Old Order laws, hide the beautiful baby dress in the attic?

Thus begins the story of Katie's painful search for the truth, one which ultimately brings her to the eternal Truth. But on the way, she endures a shunning that takes her far from her home and family....

She has already lost her first love, Daniel, and on the eve of Katie's wedding to widower Bishop John, her anguished parents reveal some startling news. Feeling betrayed, Katie watches in despair as the only life she has ever known begins to unravel. Far from Lancaster County and in the world of strangers, Katie once again is compelled to face the heritage of her past...and eventually find a future of hope.

THE PROMISE OF HEALING, THE HOPE OF NEW LOVE

The Postcard

Growing up Plain, Rachel Yoder dreamed of being a person of confidence, like her ancestors. But unlike her fiery grandfather, who spoke out against the outdated practices of the community and found himself shunned, Rachel was said to be "born shy." And then came the tragedy that stole her beloved husband away at so young an age. Now, Rachel is so shadowed by grief even her young daughter has trouble coaxing her out of her shell.

Philip Bradley's arrival at the Orchard Guest House B&B would be called providential by certain folk in the Lancaster Amish community, for it is Philip who stumbles across a forsaken postcard in the crevice of an antique desk. A world-weary journalist, Philip finds his enthusiasm renewed at the challenge the postcard presents. Written in Pennsylvania Dutch and signed by an infamous Plain relative, the faded message leads Philip to the bedside of a woman with a tale of dark secrets and lost love.

Drawn to the ancient story, Philip and Rachel find their own lives inexorably intertwined. Will their discoveries give Rachel the courage to embrace the promise of healing and the hope of new love?

The Crossroad

After the dramatic conclusion to his discovery of a long-lost postcard, journalist Philip Bradley simply cannot forget the Amish people he met while on assignment in Pennsylvania—particularly Rachel Yoder and her young daughter, Annie. Rachel's cheerful outlook, in spite of her blindness, and her appealing, uncomplicated lifestyle beckon Philip amid the high-paced existence of his New York career.

Philip's newfound knowledge of the true reason for Rachel's loss of sight spurs him on to uncover what he can about the possibility for a cure. In Lancaster County, Rachel has her own ideas about the way her vision might be restored, and it doesn't include the local hex doctor or his black bag of potions. No, Rachel firmly believes the God she serves is the only One who can grant her sight, but as the memories of the trauma she suffered begin to resurface, Rachel questions whether she can bear the agonizing road to recovery.

Drawn back to Lancaster County over the Christmas holidays, Philip struggles with the vast gulf separating him from the beautiful Plain woman. Rachel has suffered unbearable heartache; will Philip's growing affection for her only bring more of the same? Or must Philip and Rachel sacrifice a future for the sake of all they know and love?

MODERN WAYS COLLIDE WITH CHERISHED TRADITION

Lydia Cottrell, eldest of five Amish orphans, made a promise to her dying mother—to "keep the family together." But soon she discovers the guardianship has been granted to a virtual stranger—a well-to-do aunt from Portland, Oregon, who cares little for Mamma's last wish. Lydia's struggle to keep her promise may cost her the loss of "the sweetest, kindest, and most handsome Plain boy in all of Lancaster County"—Levi King.

A thoroughly modern woman, Sarah Cain had ridiculed her sister's choice of a Plain lifestyle, which served only to intensify the lifelong rift between them. Now, twelve years later, Sarah is stunned by news of her sister's death and baffled by Ivy's choice of a guardian. How can Sarah sacrifice her successful career and a life she enjoys to raise five Amish orphans? And what of Bryan Ford, the man in her life?

Upon her arrival in Lancaster County, Sarah holds a grief all her own—one very different from the suffering of her nieces and nephews. Can the sorrow that divides them ultimately unite the new family? Will Sarah discover the Lancaster County's Amish community is not only a simpler place, but also a healing place?

A Fast-Paced Page-Turner From Beverly and Her Husband, David

She had hoped this day would never come.

Trembling, Melissa James returned the phone to its cradle and hurried to the stairs. She grasped the railing, nearly stumbling as she made her way to the second-story bedroom. Her heart caught in her throat as she considered the next move. Her only option.

You can do this, *she told herself, stifling a sob.* You must....

So begins *Sanctuary,* a novel from the writing team of Beverly Lewis and her husband, David. A harrowing love story, the book captures the power that drives revenge, the price for freedom, and the solace found in friendship. Its characters are tender, flawed, and wounded, driven by a search for meaning that will bring them to a moment of shocking and profound truth.

For fear-ridden Melissa James, the roadside billboard offers the first shred of hope. Desperate for a place "where time stands still," Melissa finds safe haven amid rolling hills of idyllic Amish countryside and quaint clapboard farmhouses. It is there that she forms an unlikely alliance with a young Plain woman whose unwavering faith provides Melissa a glimpse of peace she has never known. But even there, she cannot hide.

Ryan James had it all—a beautiful wife, a lucrative investment firm, a bright future. Then his beloved Melissa disappears, leaving him both baffled and frantic. Until that day, Ryan had embraced society's blasé view of good and evil. Now, as he unravels the mystery that haunts his wife, he is faced with a depravity he cannot explain away, one that may cost him everything.

The Sunroom Becomes a Place Where Miracles Happen....

When I was twelve, I made a naïve, yet desperate, pact with God to keep my ailing mother alive. It was the first time I'd ventured something so brazen—making a contract with the Almighty....

S̶o begins the story of Becky Owens, a talented and passionate young pianist on the verge of adolescence when she learns the devastating news of her mother's critical illness. As the daughter of a country preacher in Lancaster County, Becky knows well the significance of sacrifice, and in her bargain with God, she vows to exchange her most cherished possession for her mother's life.

Hospital rules only add to Becky's sorrow—twelve-year-olds aren't allowed to visit, so Becky and her mother must share tearful smiles through Lancaster General's sunroom window. But a realization of the power of music and a lesson in unconditional love compel Becky to rethink her unusual "deal" with God....

An Exquisite Picture Book—
The Story of a Swedish Christmas

"What would I wish for?" Annika wondered aloud. "If ever I had the almond in my pudding...what would be my wish?"

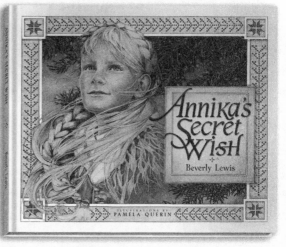

*I*n turn-of-the-century Sweden, finding the almond hidden in the rice pudding is the Christmas Eve highlight for many children, since it means a chance to wish...for a new pair of snowshoes, a mountain of truffles coated with coca, an adorable kitten. For ten long years—all of her life—Annika has dreamed of discovering the almond in her own pudding. Will this be her year?

A beautiful book that will become a part of a family's Christmas heritage, *Annika's Secret Wish* inspires young and old to freely give and share even long hoped-for gifts. The final page features Swedish Christmas traditions that families may choose to include in their own holiday celebration.

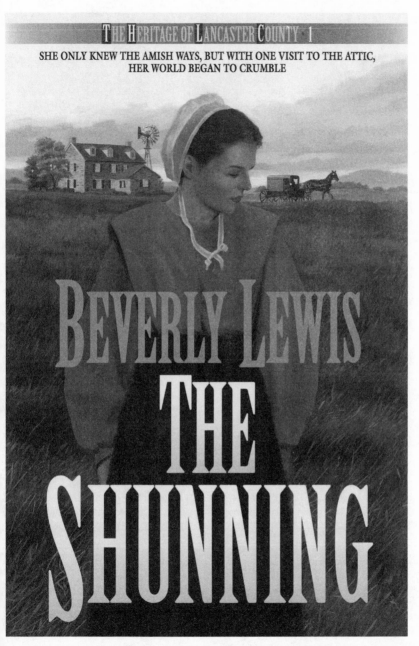

SHE ONLY KNEW THE AMISH WAYS, BUT WITH ONE VISIT TO THE ATTIC,
HER WORLD BEGAN TO CRUMBLE

BEVERLY LEWIS
THE
SHUNNING

*Turn the page for a preview of the bestselling novel about
faith and family ties in Lancaster County....*

Prologue: Katie

If the truth be known, I was more conniving than all three of my brothers put together. Hardheaded, too.

All in all, *Dat* must've given me his "whatcha-do-today-you'll-sleep-with-tonight" lecture every other day while I was growing up. But I wasn't proud of it, and by the time I turned nineteen, I was ready to put my wicked ways behind me and walk the "straight and narrow." So with a heart filled with good intentions, I had my kneeling baptism right after the two-hour Preaching on a bright September Sunday.

The barn was filled with my Amish kinfolk and friends that day three years ago when five girls and six boys were baptized. One of the girls was Mary Stoltzfus—as close as any real sister could be. She was only seventeen then, younger than most Plain girls receiving the ordinance, but as honest and sweet as they come. She saw no need in putting off what she'd always intended to do.

After the third hymn, there was the sound of sniffling. I, being the youngest member of my family and the only daughter, shouldn't have been too surprised to find that it was Mamma.

When the deacon's wife untied my *kapp*, some pigeons

251

flapped their wings in the barn rafters overhead. I wondered if it might be some sort of sign.

Then it came time for the bishop's familiar words: "Upon your faith, which you have confessed before God and these many witnesses, you are baptized in the name of the Father, the Son, and the Holy Spirit. Amen." He cupped his hands over my head as the deacon poured water from a tin cup. I remained motionless as the water ran down my hair and over my face.

After being greeted by the bishop, I was told to "rise up." A holy kiss was given me by the deacon's wife, and with renewed hope, I believed this public act of submission would turn me into an honest-to-goodness Amishwoman. Just like Mamma.

Dear *Mam*.

Her hazel eyes held all the light of heaven. Heavenly hazel, I always called them. And they were, especially when she was in the midst of one of her hilarious stories. We'd be out snapping peas or husking corn, and in a blink, her stories would come rolling off her tongue.

They were always the same—no stretching the truth with Mam, as far as I could tell. She was a stickler for honesty; fairness, too, right down to the way she never overcharged tourists for the mouth-watering jellies and jams she loved to make. Her stories, *ach*, how she loved to tell them—for the telling's sake. And the womenfolk—gathered for a quilting frolic or a canning bee—always hung on every word, no matter how often they were repeated.

There were stories from her childhood and after—how the horses ran off with her one day, how clumsy she was at needlework, and how it was raising three rambunctious boys, one after another. Soon her voice would grow soft as velvet and she'd say, "That was all back before little Katie came along"— as though my coming was a wondrous thing. And it seemed to me, listening to her weave her stories for all the rest of the women, that this must be how it'd be when the Lord God above welcomed you into His Kingdom. Mamma's love was heavenly, all right. It just seemed to pour right out of her and into me.

Then long after the women had hitched their horses to the family buggies and headed home, I'd trudge out to the barn and sit in the hayloft, thinking. Thinking long and hard about the way Mamma always put things. There was probably nothing to ponder, really, about the way she spoke of me—at least that's what Mary Stoltzfus always said. And she should know.

From my earliest memories, Mary was usually right. I was never one to lean hard on her opinion, though. Still, we did everything together. Even liked the same boys sometimes. She was very bright, got the highest marks through all eight grades at the one-room schoolhouse where all us Amish kids attended.

After eighth grade, Mary finished up with book learning and turned her attention toward becoming a wife and mother someday. Being older by two years, I had a head start on her. So we turned our backs on childhood, leaving it all behind— staying home with our mammas, making soap and cleaning house, tending charity gardens, and going to Singing every other Sunday night. Always together. That was how things had been with us, and I hoped always would be.

Mary and Katie.

Sometimes my brother Eli would tease us. "*Torment* is more like it," Mary would say, which was the honest truth. Eli would be out in the barn scrubbing down the cows, getting ready for milking. Hollering to get our attention, he'd run the words together as if we shared a single name. "Mary 'n Katie, get yourselves in here and help! Mary 'n Katie!"

We never complained about it; people knew we weren't just alike. *Jah*, we liked to wear our good purple dresses to suppers and Singing, but when it came right down to it, Mary and I were as different as a potato and a sugar pea.

Even Mamma said so. Thing is, she never put Mary in any of her storytelling. Guess you had to be family to hear your name mentioned in the stories Mam told, because family meant the world to her.

Still, no girl should have been made over the way Mamma carried on about me. Being Mam's favorite was both a blessing and a curse, I decided.

In their younger years, my brothers—Elam, Eli, and Benjamin—were more ornery than all the wicked kings in the Bible combined—a regular trio of tricksters. Especially Eli and Benjamin. Elam got himself straightened out some last year around Thanksgiving, about the time he married Annie Fisher down Hickory Lane. The responsibilities of farming and caring for a wife, and a baby here before long, would settle most any fellow down.

If ever I had to pick a favorite brother, though, most likely Benjamin would've been it. Which isn't saying much, except that he was the least of my troubles. He and that softhearted way he has about him sometimes.

Take last Sunday, for instance—the way he sat looking so forlorn at dinner after the Preaching, when Bishop Beiler and all five of his children came over to eat with us. The bishop had announced our upcoming wedding—his and mine—that day right after service. So now we were officially published. Our courting secret was out, and the People could start spreading the news in our church district, the way things had been done for three hundred years.

The rumors about all the celery Mamma and I had planted last May would stop. I'd be marrying John Beiler on Thursday, November twenty-first, and become stepmother to his five young children. And, jah, we'd have hundreds of celery sticks at my wedding feast—enough for two-hundred-some guests.

Days after the wedding was announced, Benjamin put on his softer face. Today, he'd even helped hoist me up to the attic to look for Mam's wedding dress, which I just had to see for myself before I finished stitching up my own. Ben stayed there, hovering over me like I was a little child, while I pulled the long dress out of the big black trunk. Deep blue, with a white apron and cape for purity, the dress was as pretty as an Amish wedding dress could be.

Without warning, Ben's words came at me—tumbled right out into the musty, cold air. "Didja ever think twice about marrying a widower with a ready-made family?"

I stared at him. "Well, Benjamin Lapp, that's the most ridiculous thing I've ever heard."

He nodded his head in short little jerks. "It's because of Daniel Fisher, ain't?" His voice grew softer. "Because Daniel went and got himself drowned."

The way he said it—gentle-like—made me want to cry. Maybe he was right. Maybe I was marrying John because Dan Fisher was dead—because there could never be another love for me like Dan. Still, I was stunned that Ben had brought it up.

Here was the brother who'd sat behind me in school, yank-

ing my hair every chance he got, making me clean out the
barn more times than I could count . . . and siding against me
the night Dat caught me playing Daniel's old guitar in the haymow.

But now Ben's eyes were full of questions. He was worrying
out loud about my future happiness, of all things.

I reached up and touched his ruddy face. "You don't have
to worry, brother," I whispered. "Not one little bit."

"Katie . . . for certain?" His voice echoed in the stillness.

I turned away and reached into the trunk, avoiding his
gaze. "John's a *gut* man," I said firmly. "He'll make a right fine
husband."

I felt Ben's eyes boring a hole into the back of my head,
and for a long, awkward moment he was silent. Then he replied, "Jah, right fine he'll be."

The subject was dropped. My brother and everyone else
would just have to keep their thoughts to themselves about me
and the forty-year-old man I was soon to marry. I knew well
and good that John Beiler had one important thing on his
mind: He needed a mamma for his children. And I, having
been blessed with lavish mother-love, was just the person to
give it.

Respect for a husband, after all, was honorable. In time,
perhaps something more would come of our union—John's
and mine. Perhaps even . . . love.

I could only hope and pray that my Dan had gone to his
eternal reward, and that someday I'd be found worthy to join
him there.